BARRINGTON MAGIC

SMALL TOWN ROMANCE

BARRINGTON SERIES

SUSAN MACKIE

small town
publishing

Cover Design by Susan Mackie, Small Town Publishing

ISBN: 978-1-7643186-1-7 Print Edition

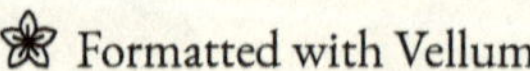 Formatted with Vellum

FOREWORD

While the town of Barrington does exist, it is little more than a small village with a general store, hall and school.

I've imagined elements of nearby larger towns, such as Gloucester, to create the township of Barrington for this story.

Any similarities to people, living or deceased, are purely co-incidental and a product of my imagination.

The Barrington Tops, Bucketts Mountain, Barrington, Dilgry and Gloucester Rivers and Jems Creek are real, and it is a stunning region to visit.

1

———

Evie - almost 6. (Four months to Christmas)

'Cᴀᴍ Jᴇɴɴɪɴɢs sᴀʏs Sᴀɴᴛᴀ's ɴᴏᴛ ʀᴇᴀʟ! Aɴᴅ ʜᴇ's ᴀ ʙɪɢ kid in grade two.' I didn't mean to blurt it out, but I wanted to take Mummy by surprise. I watched her face carefully. Sometimes her neck goes red when she's keeping a secret. But it didn't go red and she just smiled in a sweet-but-sad kind of way and knelt with her arms open.

'I really want to know the truth about Santa!' My voice wobbled as she pulled me against her. She smelt like fresh-baked bread, which is a good smell. Sometimes she smells like horses, which isn't exactly horrible, but it's not nice either.

When she didn't say anything, I tried again. 'Woz says Santa is real and he says he saw reindeer footprints in the front garden last year. But we had Christmas here too, Mummy, and I don't remember that.'

Mummy leaned back, but kept hold of my hands. Her neck wasn't red, or even pink. I waited.

'It was all a bit of a rush for us last year Evie, I'm not surprised you don't remember.' Mummy kissed the top of my head. I used to love that but I'm a big girl now, not a baby.

I frowned at her. 'Don't kiss my head.' I almost stamped my foot but the last time I did that she got upset. No. Not upset. Kinda sad. I like it better when she's all smiley and happy.

'Is. Santa. Real? I want to know, Mummy!' I had my hands on my hips and used my sternest voice. The one I use for BlueDog when he chases the chickens.

Mummy smiled when she answered. 'You know how I think all of Barrington is a little bit magic?'

I nodded. She says that a lot.

'Well, if you believe in magic, Barrington magic, why would Santa *not* be real?'

I thought about that. Why couldn't Santa be real? Woz says he is.

I nibbled my bottom lip and tried again. 'But why does Cam Jennings say he isn't real?'

Mummy sighed. But she was still smiling. 'Perhaps Cam doesn't believe in magic. It only works if you believe.'

2

———

Samantha

Curled up on the sofa beside Jamie, Samantha remembered the conversation with Evie earlier in the day, and sighed.

Jamie nudged her. 'What has you sighing? The children are asleep in their beds and we're all alone on this very cosy sofa.' As if to illustrate his point, he pulled her onto his lap. Samantha giggled, then tipped her face up. She was rewarded with a slow, gentle kiss.

'Evie. She asked about Santa again this afternoon, while you and Woz were feeding the horses.' Sam shook her head. 'Part of me wants to tell her the truth.'

Jamie raised his eyebrows but his words were soft. 'We've talked about this, Sam. She's never had a proper Christmas. One she could be excited about and look forward to. Last year was such a whirlwind, it was upon us before we had a chance to make it special for her. We said we'd give her this one, if we could, so she could experience Christmas magic at least once in her life.'

Tears formed in Samantha's eyes as she snuggled into Jamie's shoulder. 'I know. I want her to have that. The excitement, the build-up. The magic.' She shook her head. 'But some of the bigger kids at school have told her Santa isn't real. And we still have four months until Christmas.'

'They're young for such a short time, Sam.' Jamie gazed into the fireplace. 'I can still remember the anticipation I felt in the lead up to Christmas when I was little.' He kissed the tip of her nose. 'And Woz believes. He told me what Cam Jennings said to Evie, but emphatically stated that Cam has it wrong.' He chuckled and Samantha relaxed.

'Woz. He's such a good brother to Evie. I couldn't love him more.' Samantha wriggled out of Jamie's embrace. Standing, she held her hand out to him. 'Or you, Jamie Tait. Let's turn in. There's something I need you to do for me.' She gave him a look. A hot look. She'd been shy at first, but after more than six months living together, she'd begun to come into her own. The book club girls talked a lot about *the power of being women*. Some of their stories made her blush, and many made her giggle.

Jamie was on his feet in seconds. He scooped Samantha into his arms and nuzzled her neck as he carried her to their room. 'What happened to the shy young mother I met a year ago? You're quite bold these days, Sam.' He kissed her again as he lay her gently on the bed.

'I'm using my power for good, instead of evil.' Samantha giggled as she shimmied out of her jeans. Jamie had no words.

3

Hannelore

'Are you going to the Chamber of Commerce meeting tonight Mum?' Hanna poked her head out of the kitchen. 'Kristen is, and we'll stay on and have a bite of dinner at the pub afterwards.'

Millie paused, one hand hovering over the coffee machine she was wiping down. 'I was going to, but it's so quiet today, I'd be happy to close early and go out to Finn's. He's sending Lucas in for the meeting.'

Hanna frowned. 'Are you alright Mum? You look a bit hot and bothered.'

Sighing, Millie wiped her forehead with the back of her hand. 'Bloody menopause. I've been having hot flushes all day. I don't feel like sitting through a meeting tonight.'

'Oh, Mum.' Hanna walked across and patted Millie's shoulder, then giggled. 'Sorry, but is that why you were in and out of the cool room this afternoon? Kristen said she thought you were cleaning.'

Leaning against the countertop, Millie gave her a sheepish grin. 'I put that empty milk crate in there last week. I've been sneaking in and sitting on it for a few minutes, when I can.' She raised her chin. 'It helps.'

Trying not to laugh, Hanna nodded. 'We thought you were standing on it to clean the top shelves.'

'Nope. No cleaning. Just enjoying the cool air.' Millie chuckled, while fanning her face with one hand. 'But if you're going to the meeting, they won't miss me. And you can catch me up on everything tomorrow.'

'Alright. Why don't you head off Mum, we'll finish up here. The meeting doesn't start until five thirty.' Hanna paused as Kristen joined them. 'About the meeting ... they want ideas to boost visitors to town. It's been tough, with the drought going on so long.'

Millie straightened, her face had gone red again. 'The bookshop midweek tours have helped, to some extent. Maybe we need more activities for visitors that don't rely on rivers and waterfalls. She exhaled. 'Now, if you'll excuse me, I'm just going to check the light is off in the cool room.'

Millie marched out the back and Hanna and Kristen giggled when they heard her use an expletive as she closed the cool room door.

Hanna turned to Kristen. 'Our figures are down too, but thank goodness for the small weddings and events that bring in extra.'

'Hanna, I've lived here all my life and the rains will come.

They always do. We just need to ride it out.' Kristen undid her apron, bunching it in both hands. 'Turn the sign to closed, we can be done here in twenty minutes.'

THEY FOUND LUCAS AT THE BAR. 'WHAT WILL YOU HAVE girls?' He nodded towards the smaller dining room that had been set up for the meeting. 'There's a few people here already, but we've got ten minutes before it starts.'

'Red wine please Lucas.' Hanna peered across to the meeting room. 'Meggie is in there already. We may as well go in.'

'Same for me, please.' Kristen moved her tote bag from her shoulder to her hand. She was treasurer of the Chamber of Commerce and had brought her laptop.

Reaching for the glass of wine, Hanna was startled when two strong arms wrapped themselves around her from behind. Harry nuzzled the back of her neck, growling, 'Just where do you think you're going, Hanna Tucker?'

Turning carefully in his arms so her wine didn't spill, she batted him playfully. 'Chamber meeting. And I know you know that because we discussed it this morning at breakfast.' She kissed him quickly on the mouth and took a step back.

'Maybe I'll come to the meeting too. Could be more interesting than waiting for you to finish so we can have dinner.' Harry shrugged and looked over her head to Lucas.

Hanna stared at Harry, then Lucas, then back to Harry. 'The meeting? You? Why Harry Stewart? You've never shown interest in our local chamber of commerce before?'

Shrugging again, Harry spoke over her head to the barman.

'Beer please Baz.' Lucas and Kristen had begun walking toward the meeting room. Hanna waited while Harry paid for his drink, then followed the others.

Stopping, Hanna nibbled her bottom lip. 'Actually, it's really nice that you're interested. But Harry, I think you need to be a member to come to the meeting.' She frowned. 'We'll only be an hour. Just wait for us out here.'

'Yeah. Nah.' Harry opened the door to the meeting room and stood back to allow Hanna to walk in first. *Always the gentleman, Harry Stewart.*

Kristen called out. 'Come on you two. We're about to start.'

Meggie Hamilton-Masters was the President, and she waved them in. Hanna wanted to tell Harry to wait at the bar, but Meggie was already speaking as he slid into the chair next to her.

Hanna noted a bigger turnout than usual. The main item of business was the drought, and how all the main street businesses were struggling. Some had already laid off casual staff, with business owners working longer hours themselves.

The owner of the bakery, Merv Andrews, raised his hand. 'We're working seven days, Meggie, now that we've had to let some staff go. I've spoken to a few others here, and we think we should go back to the trading hours we had before.'

Hanna was confused. She mouthed *before?* to Kristen, who gave her an I-don't-know look.'

Ben Evans cleared his throat, and all heads turned to him. 'Do you mean trading until noon on Saturday and closed on Sunday, Merv?'

'Yes. Exactly. A lot of us are owner-operators and the effect of the drought is making us work longer hours, for less income.

We're struggling. And that's not just because visitation is down, but locals are doing it tough and not spending as much either. For those of us without staff, we need a day off. Weekend trade is not covering casual wages.' Merv folded his arms across his chest.

Hanna raised her hand.

'Yes Hanna?' Meggie smiled encouragingly.

'I understand if some, like you Merv,' she gave him a nod, 'want to reduce trading hours. And of course it's your choice. But it would be our choice, or Millie's choice anyway, to keep the café open. It worries me that if a large portion of the main street businesses choose to close, the word might get around, via social media and so on, that Barrington doesn't open after twelve on Saturday. And I think that would further discourage visitors.' She felt a slight pressure from Harry's leg against hers. From the corner of her eye, she saw him nod. 'And once it does rain, building business back up with mixed messages in the marketplace, may be harder.'

'Accommodation places, like The Lofts, would struggle to sell their Saturday nights if there is nowhere to get breakfast or coffee on Sunday.' Ben shifted in his seat, speaking directly to Merv. 'It would set us back twenty years, Merv.'

Merv sighed, and hung his head. 'I know Ben. But we're struggling if we work every day ourselves, and going backwards if we use casual staff at the weekend.'

In the end Merv didn't move a motion to restrict main street trade and the meeting ended with everyone promising to look for ways to boost visitation while they wait for the drought to break.

Leaving the meeting, Harry took her hand in his. 'I'm hungry, let's get a table. Lucas is staying too, and Kristen.'

'Sure Harry, I'm hungry.' *And a bit despondent.* Hanna

worried for Merv and his wife. They had a great business but they were close to retirement age. She understood their dilemma but agreed completely with Ben that it would set their little town back years. Decades.

4

____

Harry

Harry could feel Hanna's gaze on him as they settled into a booth and picked up the menus.

'Anyone fancy sharing pizzas tonight?' Kristen pointed to the menu. "Maybe a garlic and two others?'

'I'm in.' Lucas was quick to answer and Harry was pleased when Hanna readily agreed. They chose quickly and Lucas went to order. He was getting drinks too, and they'd split the bill at the end.

When they were all settled, Harry nudged Lucas and grinned at Hanna and Kristen. 'Ladies, we've got something we want to tell you. Lucas and I have an idea. For a business.'

'What?' Hanna raised her eyebrows. 'You already have a business, with your Dad. Building.' She turned to Lucas. 'And so do you, with your Dad at the winery.'

'And you have a business too, Hannelore Tucker. And you

work with your Mum in the café.' Harry was miffed. He'd though she'd be excited for him.

As if she could read his mind, she laughed out loud. 'You're right, I do.' She grinned at him and across at Lucas. 'Okay...spill. What are two of my favourite blokes up to? What's your idea?'

Harry took a deep breath. He and Lucas had discussed it several times in the last two weeks, and he'd thought about it a lot. He'd messaged Lucas today and they were keen to see Hanna and Kristen's reactions. They hadn't told their fathers...yet. 'Wine tours.' Hanna looked confused and glanced at Kristen.

'Go on.' Kristen leaned forward, so Harry focussed on her as he spoke.

'Actually, the idea came about because we were chatting about the affect the drought was having on businesses. We were throwing ideas around about activities for visitors that don't need fast flowing rivers and waterfalls to hike to.'

Lucas chimed in. 'We were thinking about that demographic. You know, younger people, groups of friends and couples who like kayaking and touring to see waterfalls. And we don't get a lot of them, that demographic, at Barrington Ridge Wines. Mostly slightly older couples and friends who are in the area for the scenic stuff, but also the wine, beer and local produce.'

'And why don't young people.' He winked at Hanna. 'Our age, do cellar door tours?'

'Um. They're not wine drinkers?' Hanna still looked perplexed.

'Maybe they're not. Maybe they're still learning about wines.' Harry sipped the beer in front of him. 'Like me. I only started taking an interest in wine when I met you, Hanna, and Finn and

Lucas. But I was unsure about wine at the start. You know, how do I tell if it's good or not?' He shrugged.

'And we think a lot of younger people, blokes like us, would feel like that. And maybe their girlfriends have a more sophisticated palate.' Lucas picked up the glass of red in front of Hanna, raised it towards the light, swirled it, then eyed it critically. 'Smooth red, tannins in the bottom of the glass.' He took a sip. 'A hint of berry as it hits the back of the tongue.'

Hanna reached across, removing the glass from his hand. 'Just as well we're almost family Lucas. No one messes with my wine.' She returned the glass to the table. 'But I get it, and I think you're right. Young people don't want to do a tour with a bunch of older, er, wine snobs. They want to have fun, possibly learn a bit, but not be out of their depth.' She nodded at Harry.

'But it might not be the best time to start a new business, with the drought affecting trade. Visitation is down more than fifty percent.'

Kristen leaned forward. 'Hold on Hanna. Starting a business at a low time can be a good thing. If they can build the business slowly, with low overheads and, you know, try out their ideas. By the time the rain comes and the tourists are back in numbers, they'll have their business model right.'

'And that's the sort of advice we need Kristen.' Harry looked at Lucas, who nodded. 'Will you be our accountant? On the books? We're putting in some seed money to get started.'

Bouncing in her seat a little bit, Kristen nodded enthusiastically. She clapped her hands. 'Yes! I will. Tell us more. What do you need to get started?'

'The name.' Harry nudged Hanna. 'We have some ideas, but you're good at this. And a bit of help with branding, website and marketing. We'll register for an ABN as soon as we've locked the name in.'

'What are you thinking? For the business name?' Hanna rested her chin on her steepled fingers. Harry was sure she was beginning to see the possibilities.

'***Wine for Blokes. Unpretentious wine and food tours in Barrington.***' Harry sat back, hoping he looked nonchalant. He and Lucas had been drinking together when they came up with the name, but it still rang true for Harry, even in the light of day.

'Oh gosh!' Hanna clapped a hand to her mouth, stifling a laugh. 'That's fun...and funny...and clever.' She leaned over and kissed Harry loudly on the mouth. 'Mwah! I'd do that tour! The name says it all!'

'Brilliant!' Kristen picked up her wine. 'The pizzas are here. Let's chat while we eat. I'm starving!'

Harry demolished a slice of garlic pizza, then a gourmet chicken piece. He pointed to the pizzas. 'We're thinking small groups, maximum of ten. Breakfast at the café, then the cheese place on the other side of town. Lunch at Barrington Ridge wines with an informal tasting. Drive them back to town via a lookout, through the state forest. Then recommend dinner here at the pub. We can do full day, half day and two-day tours. But we need a minimum of four people.' He pushed the pizza closer to Kristen. 'That's where you come in. To make sure we have our costings right.' He took another slice himself, this time the prosciutto and rocket. His favourite. It had a swirl of caramelised balsamic across the top. 'And you Hanna, can you help with the price points? How to create packages to make it attractive.'

Hanna was frowning. 'Up to ten people. You'll need a minibus. Have you factored that in?'

'Actually, we've already got a vehicle lined up that we think will work.' Lucas slid another slice onto his plate. 'Harry has been offered a Landcruiser Troop Carrier. Four-wheel drive, eleven seats.'

'A troop carrier?' Hanna looked confused.

'Neil Jennings has one for sale. It has bench seats in the back, for eight, and three seats in the front. Now that his older boys have their licences, he doesn't need the extra seating. It's in good condition, the price is right, and it's white, so it will be easy to add signage on the sides and back.' Harry watched her face. She was processing, then he saw her slowly nod.

'So just weekends then, to begin with?' Kristen was making notes on her phone, her plate pushed away.

'No. We're going to try for a mid-week tour, even just one day. Lucas will do that, when the Cellar Door is quiet. And I'll keep my job with Dad, but will do the weekend tours.' Harry smiled at Hanna. 'You work a lot at weekends too, so it shouldn't affect, um, us.'

Kristen looked at her watch. 'I must go. I promised to call Callum.' She looked up. 'Is it okay to tell him, about this?'

'Yes. But ask him to keep it to himself for now.' Harry scratched his chin. 'We need a meeting with you Kristen, to set up the accounts. We're putting seed money into a partnership account and we'll use that to buy the vehicle.'

Kristen slid out of the booth, picked up her tote bag, then paused, looking directly at Lucas. 'Callum told me last night that Freddie is coming home next month. She hopes to get some work at the Vet Clinic with Angus and Max.' She placed her hand lightly on his shoulder. 'I thought you should know.'

Lucas nodded and smiled. 'Thanks Kristen. Good to know. Yeah. Good. Thanks.'

Harry could see his friend had been taken by surprise and wondered if he still had feelings for Freddie. Harry hoped he didn't. Freddie was shamelessly wicked and she'd broken Lucas's heart last time.

Wanting to take the attention off Lucas, who had gone pale, Harry turned to Hanna. 'And the branding? Should I ask Laura for a logo? Or Meggie?'

Hanna nodded, then wiped her fingers on a serviette. She picked up her wine glass and finished it. 'Why don't we go home to my place Harry, and I can muck around with some ideas on my laptop? Do you want to come over too, Lucas?'

Lucas stood up. 'I'll get the bill.' He grinned at Harry. 'Wine for Blokes will cover this. It was a business strategy meeting.' He shook his head then. 'I'm going home too. If you and Hanna come up with some ideas, just shoot them through to me.'

Something about Lucas's posture had Harry groaning inwardly. *Oh no, he still has feelings for Freddie.*

As they walked across the road to Hanna's apartment in the top of the post office building, Harry wondered, not for the first time, when they might make a home of their own. Together.

5

Finn

'I'LL OPEN THE WINDOW, TO LET SOME COOL AIR IN.'
Finn moved to the other side of the room, keeping an eye on
Millie as he went. Her face was flushed, she looked uncomfortable
and she had been unusually quiet during dinner. Then she'd
snapped at him when he moved close to her on the couch, telling
him it was too hot to cuddle. Finn knew it was less than ten
degrees outside, and while the living room was warm enough, he'd
kept a light jumper on over his shirt. Millie, on the other hand,
was wearing a tee shirt and yoga pants.

Millie had told him she was menopausal a few weeks ago. He'd
googled it. His Doctor Google investigations pointed more to
peri-menopause but he wasn't prepared to mention it. Not right
now, anyway. She'd also said she didn't want to take medication,
but he hoped she might reconsider that. She was obviously
suffering.

'Thank you Finn.' Millie fanned a magazine in front of her face for a moment. 'I've been like this all day. Fine one moment, molten lava the next.' She grimaced. 'Maybe I should head home.'

'Don't go, Millie. I'll make you a lime and soda. With ice.' He smiled sympathetically and walked to the kitchen when she nodded.

'Maybe extra ice in a glass by itself!' she called out.

'Extra ice it is.' Finn carried the drink and a small bowl of ice cubes out to her. He had a half-finished glass of red wine beside his seat. 'Now, where were we?'

'Discussing the Chamber of Commerce meeting. Is this the first time Lucas has gone, in your place, Finn?' Millie picked up an ice cube and dribbled it down the front of her shirt. Finn tried not to stare. She looked hot. And she looked *hot*.

Leaning back, he focussed on his wine for a moment. 'Actually, I think the young bloke may have his own reason for attending tonight.' He cocked an eyebrow at Millie.

'Really?'

'He and Harry Stewart have been as thick as thieves for a couple of weeks now. I suspect he has a business idea. Or maybe he's helping Harry with something new.' He sipped his wine, then placed the glass back on the side table. 'Has Hanna mentioned anything?'

Millie brought the tall tumbler, dripping with condensation, to her cheek. 'Not a word. If Harry's involved, then I don't think he's told her.' She raised the glass to her mouth and drank more than half of it down, then topped it up with ice from the bowl. She closed her eyes for a moment. 'So cool. Mmmm.'

Finn shifted in his seat. 'Making noises like that won't keep you cool, Millie.' Her eyes flew open and she giggled. He grinned back.

'Being hot for a reason is different.' Millie waved a hand up and down her body. 'This heat is just another physical challenge women have to face. As if we don't have enough to deal with already.' She must have seen the look on his face, because she hesitated, then added more softly. 'Of course, none of this is your fault, Finn.'

Cocking his head on one side, Finn glanced at Millie. 'Sounds like Luke's home. He might come up, he'll see the light is still on.'

Straightening her clothes, Millie sat up. 'Of course he should come up. He can tell us about the meeting. And what it is he's up to.'

LATER, FINN WAS PROPPED UP ON THE BED, HIS LEGS under the covers, while Millie sat by the partly-open window. She was hot again. He smirked to himself. *This time it was his fault.*

'Are you cold Finn? I'll close it in a moment.' Millie had on an oversize tee shirt. One of his. And nothing else. She looked so cute in it, he felt himself rousing again. Millie must have noticed because she shook a finger at him. 'No Finn. I've cooled down. You're not getting me all hot and sweaty again. There's a water shortage and I can't take another shower before morning.'

Feeling sheepish, he drew a breath. 'Alright. Let's talk about something other than how sexy you look right now.' He waggled his eyebrows and she laughed, closing the window and returning to the bed. Well, she was *on* the bed, while he was *in* the bed.

'So the boys are starting a business?' Millie framed it as a question, but before he could comment she added, 'Wine for Blokes. I like it.'

'I do too.' Finn turned toward her. 'They've thought it through, there's a gap in the market and it's a great add-on to our business here at the winery.'

'It's good for the café too. I'm sure Hanna will be keen.' Millie slid her legs under the covers. 'Harry surprised me. He's very outdoorsy and I know he's a good builder and loves working with Robbie.'

'Yeah, I wondered about Harry too. But he's become good mates with Lucas and I suspect he was looking for something extra to do on weekends when Hanna is often at her busiest.' Finn switched off the bedside lamp on his side. 'They're starting with low overheads during a quiet period. If it's successful they may be able to employ one or two others when visitation picks up.'

Millie switched her lamp off and moved closer to Finn. 'I'm impressed with it actually. And both lads have the right personalities for dealing with customers. You couldn't meet two nicer, more easy-going young men.'

Finn leaned over and kissed Millie. She relaxed into him, wrapping her arms around his neck. 'I'm changing the subject now Millie.'

'I know Finn. Stop talking.'

6

____

Freddie

Freddie spun around. The sound of his riding boots on the timber verandah outside her room was unmistakable.

'I hear you're leaving us next month?' Bartholemew Sterling leaned against the door jamb, nudging the door further open with the tip of one highly polished boot.

'What if I am?' Freddie snarled, knowing her face was flushing with embarrassment even as she willed it not to. *Bloody Bart!*

'Is it because of me, Frederica?' He raised an eyebrow, then gazed around her room. It was messy and he'd seen it before, many times. Her room was always messy. She couldn't see the sense in putting her clean laundry away when she was only going to wear it again. Freddie had never cared what anyone thought. Until now.

'Don't flatter yourself, Bartholomew.' He hated his full name as much as she hated hers. 'I'm needed at home.' Raising her chin she added, 'the local Vet Clinic has offered me a position.' It wasn't a complete lie. Angus had said he could give her casual work to start with, as business was quiet because of the drought.

Bart straightened and chuckled. It was obvious he knew it wasn't the truth. The drought in Barrington was even worse than out here in the west of the state. But she'd be damned if she'd stay a moment longer than her contract required.

Freddie glared at him as he continued to linger at the edge of her room. His gaze wandered to her bed. They'd spent many a happy hour in there together. Hours she'd rather not remember. Now.

As if reading her mind, he took a step toward her and Freddie held her hand up. 'Stop. This is my room and you're not welcome here.'

Returning to the doorway, he resumed his position. 'Technically it's my room, Frederica Campbell. I think you're forgetting that.'

Her temper flared. 'Technically.' She almost spat the word out. 'It's your father's room, Bartholemew Sterling. I think you're forgetting that!' That caught him off-guard and he shifted, standing upright. His jaw tightened. She knew he hated being reminded that his father owned the station, paid their wages, ran the stock. *Made the decisions.* When his father was away Bart liked to strut around as if it was already his.

'You little ...' He stepped towards her but Freddie held her ground.

'Little what, Bart?' Her tummy rolled over but she wasn't about to step back.

Bart smirked. 'Oh, I've got lots of names for you, Frederica. You can be quite a nasty piece of work yourself.' He folded his arms across his broad chest. 'But you must have known it would come to an end. You're not quite, er, in my league, are you?'

Further angered, Freddie took a step closer. 'No, I'm not in your league Bart. I'm way out of your league, way better than you!' She took a deep breath. 'Victoria is welcome to you.'

Laughing, Bart stepped back. 'Oh, Freddie. You've given me the time of my life. You're like a kitten one minute and a bronc-riding-cowgirl the next.' He let his gaze rove over her, from the tip of her dusty boots, long denim-clad legs and tight tee shirt to her long, curly red hair. 'And yes, Victoria Carter is welcome to me. And my family. Now that she's home from Europe we'll be announcing our engagement. I hope you'll be here for the party.' He waited a heartbeat, maybe two and when she continued to glare at him he abruptly turned, striding along the bunkhouse verandah away from her.

In two steps Freddie reached the door, and only just managed to stop herself from slamming it. She wouldn't give him the satisfaction. Picking up her phone, she sat on the edge of her bed and called her brother, Callum.

'Freddie!' Callum always sounded pleased to hear from her.

'I need to come home, Cal.' Freddie tried to keep her emotions in check. 'I know I've only got another three weeks here, but I'd like to come home now. Today. Tomorrow.'

Freddie waited. Callum always considered his words before he spoke, unlike her. It was one of the things she loved about him. 'Freddie, you know Mum and Dad will say you need to finish your contract.'

Falling back on to the bed, quietly, she agreed. 'I know. I will.' She sighed.

'You can call me anytime Freddie. If you're feeling flat, just call me.'

She wanted to tell her brother she loved him. Instead she tried to inject some enthusiasm into her voice. 'How's Kristen?'

'She's great. Better than great.' Callum's tone held so much warmth when he spoke of his girlfriend, that Freddie hoped someone would speak about her like that one day. If she was lucky.

'Good. You know I'll be your best man when you get married, don't ya Callum?' It was a running joke between them. They had five older brothers Callum could choose from, and his best mate Harry Stewart.

'You'd look better in a suit than any of them Freddie. Be careful what you wish for.' Callum laughed and Freddie realised he didn't say *it's too early for that*, or *don't get ahead of me*. Maybe he was seriously thinking about marriage. He was only eighteen months older than her.

'See ya Callum. And thanks.' Freddie ended the call. She lay on her bed for a moment, wondering if she could skip tonight's barbecue with all the station hands, managers and owners of Sterling Station.

Bart-bloody-Sterling would be swanning around with his girlfriend Victoria. And she'd be dressed in designer-something-or-other with her sleek blonde hair and her pert little nose in the air. Most of the staff knew Freddie had been messing around with the boss's son, some had even warned her against it. But Freddie had been confident that her passion matched Bart's and he would consider her a better option than Victoria. Only last night when Victoria arrived had she realised he'd been using her. Laughing at her behind her back. Taking what he wanted with no thought of the consequences.

Freddie had been guilty of that herself, in the past...Lucas. The way she had treated him, then tried to seduce Harry Stewart, made her hang her head in shame. She wanted to return to Barrington, she had nowhere else to go. But would she be welcome?

7
___

Evie (three months to Christmas)

'WAIT! WOZ, PLEASE WAIT.' I DIDN'T MEAN TO CRY, BUT my knee was sore where I fell over at lunch time and my school bag was heavy. Woz had jumped off the bus first and was already running up the lane to our house. He was excited because we were on holidays for two weeks. But I was tired and I didn't want him to get home before me. We usually walk home together.

Woz stopped running and turned around. 'Come on Evie!' He shouted but didn't come back to help me. I threw my schoolbag down and sat on it. My knee was hurting. I touched the band-aid Miss Rogers had put on and a little bit of blood trickled out. I sniffled and wiped my nose on my sleeve. I was crying for real now and covered my face with my hands, but I sneaked a peek through my fingers. Woz was standing exactly where he'd stopped.

'Come on Evie. It's holidays. Nanna will have baked something for us up at the big house.' He called out loudly and sounded cross but started walking back to me. I thought about what Nanna might have baked. Chocolate chip muffins are my favourite. I stood up, put my hand on the strap of my backpack and took a few slow steps towards him, dragging my bag in the dirt. He sighed and shook his head. Then he ran to me and picked up my bag with one hand and grabbed my hand with the other. He had his own bag over his shoulder.

I smiled at him then. 'Thank you Woz, you're the best.'

'And you're a pain.' He still sounded cross and I tried to pull my hand from his, but he held it tightly. 'Is your knee very sore?' I nodded and we kept walking. He held my hand more gently now. I could see our house up ahead but it felt further away than usual.

Then we heard the quad bike coming, and I saw BlueDog racing towards us. We stopped and BlueDog ran around us in a big circle, with a doggy-smile on his face. He wriggled and wagged his tail and then we were sitting on the track with him in our arms, licking our hands and anything else he could reach.

Jamie stopped the quad bike in front of us. 'Last day of term kids! What are you going to do with two weeks holidays?' He threw our school bags into the crate on the back of the bike then picked me up first. I always sat in front of him and Woz sat behind. Sometimes BlueDog jumped into the crate, but he couldn't today 'cos our bags were in there.

'Do you want to come home and change or should we go straight up to Nanna's?' Jamie shouted over the noise of the bike, so I shouted back. 'Nanna's!' Woz did the same. Jamie drove really fast across the paddock to the big house and I laughed out loud, closing my eyes with the wind in my face. We skid-stopped behind the house and Jamie lifted me down. I ran to the back step with

Woz and pulled off my shoes when Mummy and Nanna opened the door. I could smell muffins.

'Wash your hands, both of you.' Nanna pretended to smack us with a wooden spoon as we ran past her to the laundry tub. We giggled.

'You too, Jamie Tait.' Mummy laughed as she said it and suddenly all my tiredness left me and my knee didn't hurt. I grinned at Woz as we stood on our special step to reach the laundry tub. Mummy turned the tap on and pointed to the soap. 'I saw you sitting on the ground with BlueDog, make sure you use soap please.'

I looked at her quickly. I didn't know she could see us from here. She smiled then. 'Is that a band-aid on your knee, Evie? I'll have a look at that once you've had afternoon tea.'

Woz stepped down and dried his hands, then passed the towel to me. 'Evie fell over at lunch time, Sam. It was bleeding and she was really brave.' I felt warm on the inside when he said that and finished drying my hands, then followed Mummy and Woz through the kitchen to the big table where Pa sat. I ran to him for a quick cuddle and he whispered, 'chocolate chip muffins and lamingtons today.' I'm not sure why he whispered 'cos it wasn't a secret. I could see lots of muffins and lamingtons and biscuits piled high on plates. I high-fived Pa. He liked to do that.

After we ate, Pa held my hand while Mummy looked at my sore knee. She said it was a gravel rash and Nanna had to fetch a pair of tweezers to get the little pieces of gravel out. It hurt a lot but Pa read me a story and told me to close my eyes. So when Mummy said it was all fixed I saw my knee had a bigger band aid on it and she showed me a saucer holding the three teeny stones she'd pulled out. Nanna said it would heal quickly now it was properly cleaned and she put some of the baked treats in a container for us to take back to our house. Pa said he was going to have a chocolate muffin for dessert, heated up with ice cream on it. I thought he said that so Mummy would know what to do with ours after dinner.

I rode home with Jamie on the quad while Mummy and Woz walked across the paddock. We had the chocolate muffins for dessert just the way Pa said we should. I decided it was my best day. Ever.

8

———

Hannelore

'DID YOU SEE THAT EMAIL FROM THE CHAMBER THIS morning?' Kristen turned the sign on the door to OPEN then followed Hanna into the kitchen.

'No. I haven't checked my emails today. What's it about?' Hanna peered out from the kitchen. 'Oh, hang on. Angus is here for his coffee.' She tied an apron on as she strode to the front counter, smiling. 'Morning Angus, your usual?'

The coffee machine was already on and Hanna silently thanked Kristen. She wondered for a brief moment where Millie was, she was usually here before opening.

'Good morning Hanna. Yes please, and one for Max too.' He glanced at the tray of cakes and slices in Kristen's hands as she appeared from the kitchen. She began filling up the front cake display. 'Hi Kristen.' Angus grinned and pointed to the array of goodies. 'They look good. How about two of those as well.'

Kristen laughed and raised her eyebrows. 'The chocolate croissants? Hanna made them last night and I baked them this morning. They're still warm.'

'They don't get any fresher than that! We're having a partners' meeting before we open the clinic in an hour.' He grinned as he took custody of the bag of baked goods in one hand, and the two coffees in the other. 'And we need to get rid of the evidence before Melanie arrives, she keeps telling us we eat too many sweet things.'

Hanna laughed. 'Too funny. But they're not bad Angus, and you and Max will work off the calories.' She leaned closer now. 'They're home-made, so that means they're good for you.'

Angus rushed out, saying loudly, 'can't fault your logic, Hanna Tucker.'

Turning back to Kristen, Hanna pulled her phone from her pocket. 'The email from Chamber?'

'Nope. You'll have to wait. Incoming.' Kristen dashed back to the kitchen, leaving Hanna to greet their latest customers.

The early morning rush over, Hanna was cleaning tables when Millie arrived. Straightening, she looked at her mother, standing awkwardly by the counter. Hanna walked across, speaking quietly. 'Hi Mum. Are you okay?'

Millie gave a small smile, nodded, then moved behind the counter. Hanna followed, not sure what this was about.

'I'm sorry Hanna. Have you been under the pump without me?' Millie seemed anxious and Hanna shook her head.

'Nothing we couldn't handle. Busy, but steady.' She patted Millie on her shoulder. 'You can be late, Mum. The world won't come to an end.' She nibbled her lip. 'But are you feeling okay?'

Millie sighed, and the worry lines around her eyes lessened.

'I'm not sleeping well.' She waved a hand in front of her face and neck. 'I get hot. Sweaty. It wakes me up.'

Hanna nodded. She really didn't know much about menopause, but maybe she should google it and see if there was anything she could do to relieve her Mum's symptoms. 'Oh Mum.' She hoped she sounded sympathetic.

'They don't tell us about it. Not really.' Millie leaned against the counter, arms folded across her chest. 'And all the reading I did, well, it seems it's different for every woman, so there's no way to anticipate the symptoms. Or how severe they might be.' She grimaced. 'Finn slept in the spare room most of the night. I know I was keeping him awake, but I honestly think he did it so I would get some sleep.'

'Finn is a good man, Mum.' Hanna gazed around. A group of people were hovering just outside the door. 'It looks like a small group is coming in. But Mum, we're fine. We can manage. Go home and rest, it might do you good.'

Millie laughed suddenly and drew Hanna in for a quick, tight hug. 'Oh darling girl. I'm fine. Thank you for managing without me this morning.' She peered into the kitchen and waved good morning to Kristen and chuckled. 'And if I get hot I'll pop into the cool room.'

IT WAS AFTER TWO WHEN HANNA AND KRISTEN TOOK A break and had lunch at a table in the back. Millie had seemed fine and as far as Hanna could tell was her usual cheerful self. She had seen her come out of the cool room earlier, but only once.

'The email from Chamber, Kristen. Should I read it, or can

you give me the overview?' Hanna took a large bite of her chicken satay wrap.

'I'll get it up on my phone, Hanna.' Kristen sipped her iced tea, then fiddled with her phone a bit. She paused, reading to herself. Hanna gave her a questioning look, but took another bite of her wrap while she waited.

'Gosh, Hanna. There are a heap of responses to the first email.' Kristen looked up. 'A few people have their knickers in a knot.'

'Really?' Hanna was bemused. 'Start from the start, Kristen.'

'Maybe you should just read them.' Kristen passed her phone across. Hanna wiped her fingers on a napkin then took the phone.

The missus and I need a break. The bakery will be closed from twelve on Saturday and all day Sunday until we get rain. Merv.

Hanna glanced at Kristen. 'The bakery. That's disappointing.'

Bloody hell Merv. I thought we decided at Chamber to stay open. My business is right next to yours, so this affects me as well!! Shelley's Gifts.

Selfish move Merv. Trev.

Tough decision Merv, and of course every business may decide their own hours, but the Chamber was hoping to create a unified approach for the benefit of all local businesses. Meggie Hamilton-Masters.

Hi Merv, I totally understand and of course it's a business decision only you can make for yourself. Having said that, Council is investigating some drought relief funding. We'll know more next week, if you can hold on to the regular hours a bit longer. I will advise the Chamber President of the details when we have them to hand, so this can be disbursed to all members. Cr Ben Evans.

Thank you Ben. We'll hang on until next week for more details. Merv.

Why wasn't this mentioned last night Ben? Council filtering information through to us in a need-to-know basis like we're 5-year-olds, as usual! Trev.

When will the meeting minutes be sent out? We missed the meeting. Nadia & Frank, Barrington General Store.

'This one just popped in Kristen, about the minutes.' Hanna pointed to the message.

'I sent them to Meggie last night, to check before I send them out. She said she was waiting on something from Ben. So that's obviously the drought relief stuff.' Kristen tapped the phone. 'I'll message Meggie privately to check if I can send the minutes. We can do a separate email once we have the details on the grants.'

Picking up her own phone, Hanna opened the email trail. She nibbled her lip, and looked towards the counter where Millie was chatting with a customer. 'Should I weigh into this?'

'I wouldn't. Wait until the information comes through from Ben.' Kristen lay her phone on the table and finished her iced tea.

Hanna gathered their lunch plates and glasses onto a tray. 'You know what? I'm going to pop down to the bakery and ask Merv to make the apple strudels for that birthday event next weekend.'

'I thought you were going to do them yourself?' Kristen walked back to the kitchen beside Hanna.

'I was. But Harry asked me to come on the 'test run' in the troopie for Wines for Blokes on Saturday afternoon and I said I couldn't. But if Merv makes the strudels, I can.' Hanna nudged Kristen. 'You've got Callum coming too, haven't you? And Lucy will be here at the café so Mum will be okay.' She grinned, taking off her apron. 'I'm going to duck down to the bakery now, then I'll call Harry.'

9

Harry

AFTER CLEANING THE TROOP CARRIER INSIDE AND OUT until it gleamed in the morning sunshine, Harry stood back and admired the vehicle. He couldn't wait for the signage to arrive, Hanna had designed it herself and he and Lucas loved it.

Equal parts nervous and excited about the Wine for Blokes soft launch today, Harry was chuffed Hanna had juggled her workload to come too. He intended to drive, with Lucas in the front with him. They had created a script, of sorts, but he hoped they could wing it with their local knowledge.

Kristen and Callum were joining them. Callum was their target market. He was a beer man and confessed he was keen to learn a bit more about wine. Meggie was coming, to provide some general feedback to inform their marketing, and Judith, who was retired but managed the local bookstore. Hanna had suggested he include Judith, as she had a steady stream of senior ladies coming on the train midweek for the book store program of writers-in-residence. He wasn't sure it would appeal to that market, but Judith was awesome and he valued her input.

'You'll wash the paint off, son, if you polish it anymore.' Harry hadn't heard Robbie approach.

'She looks good, don't ya think Dad?' Harry stepped back, shoulder to shoulder with his father.

'It was a good buy, for sure.' Robbie seemed to hesitate. 'How many have you got today? Nervous?'

'Me and Lucas. Then five others, including Hanna.' Harry gave his father a sideways glance. 'More excited than nervous. And keen to get feedback from today's run.'

'So you're not full?' Robbie bent down to pat Scout, who was leaning against his leg.

'No. We can fit eight in the back and even another in the front. Someone small, like Hanna.' Harry stepped back to the car and gave the side mirror a quick polish. Robbie didn't answer and it suddenly occurred to Harry that he was waiting. 'Um, would you be interested yourself, Dad?' He turned to meet his father's gaze.

'I would, son.' Robbie grinned then. 'Nik and I think you've really hit on something. A clever idea. If you have room, I'm keen to come along. If I'm not in the way, of course.'

'Does Nik want to come too? She's welcome too.' Harry moved behind the car and opened the back door. He wondered for a moment if Judith would have trouble getting in there, she had a bad knee. He might have to put her in the front and Lucas could sit in the back.

'Nah mate. She's got guests checking in and she'll pick Lucy up from the café after work.' Robbie started to move off. 'I'll put a clean shirt on. What time are we leaving?'

'Half nine. Lucas is meeting us here. We're picking Judith and Meggie up from the train station, just to see how that works. And Hanna, Kristen and Callum from the café.' Harry looked down at his own shirt. 'If it goes well, we're going to order some merch with our logo on.'

'Merch?' Robbie slowed while Harry caught up, then they walked to the house together.

'Yeah. Shirts for Lucas and me. But also tee shirts, fleecy lined jumpers and maybe caps.' Harry chuckled. 'Who would've thought, Dad? Me, starting a tourism business.'

'You can do anything, Harry. I've always said that.' Robbie laughed loudly. 'But I think this is Hanna's influence. She's quite the entrepreneur herself.'

Harry had to agree. 'She's amazing, Dad. I'm very lucky.'

'You're both lucky.' They were in the house now and Robbie bounded up the stairs.

HARRY WAS RIGHT, THE BIG STEP UP INTO THE BACK OF the vehicle was difficult for Judith, so he settled her in the front seat with him, while Lucas jumped in the rear with Meggie and Robbie.

Parking outside the café, Harry watched Hanna, Kristen and Callum walk out. Lucas opened the back door from the inside, but got out to help the girls in.

'It's a bit of a step up, isn't it?' Hanna spoke to Lucas, then waved to Harry once she was inside. 'Hi Harry. Hello Judith, you've got the right spot, up front there.'

'I couldn't manage the step.' Judith grimaced. 'My knee.'

Lucas closed the back door and settled back in as Harry moved off slowly.

Callum cleared his throat. 'I think I could rig something up for you, Luke.' Harry glanced in the rear mirror, then concentrated on the road ahead.

'Rig something up?' Lucas said what Harry was thinking.

'A step. Like in a caravan. It could fold up when the door is closed.' Callum paused. 'I'd be happy to fit it for you.'

'Oh that's brilliant, don't you think so Kristen?' Hanna's enthusiasm was infectious.

'Yes!' Kristen was on board now. 'Could you really do it, Cal?'

'Sure. I'll measure up what we need, find the right step and mechanism online from caravan suppliers. Half a day, maximum, once I have everything.' Callum sounded sure.

Lucas caught Harry's eye in the mirror and Harry nodded. 'Sure Callum. Thanks mate. That would be awesome. We'll pay you, of course.'

'Just the materials, lads. Happy to help.' Callum spoke firmly and Harry nodded. But he didn't miss the look of pleasure on Kristen's face. She was now the accountant for Wine for Blokes and Harry thought to himself that Callum was doing it as much for her, as for them. He was offering his support in the best way he knew how. Harry swallowed the lump that came to his throat.

Judith reached over and patted his shoulder gently. 'Everyone's behind you Harry. You and Luke. I'm predicting this little business will be a runaway success.'

Sweet Judith. Nicest lady in Barrington. Harry nodded at her, then grinned as he heard Lucas launch into tour guide mode. He focussed on the road, only glancing occasionally in the mirror. Lucas was in his element and he chuckled when Hanna asked questions, pretending she wasn't a local. A quick peek at Judith told him she was enjoying it too and now they were all asking questions.

They stopped on the southern side of Rocky Crossing, stepping out for a look at the water, barely crossing the causeway, it was so low. But Lucas pointed to the high-water markers and told anecdotes about tourists who had been caught when the water was higher, with their vehicles washed into the rushing river.

After returning to the vehicle they headed towards Barrington Ridge Wines. Finn was doing the first wine tasting with them, followed by a barbecue, with salads and desserts provided by the café.

They had another winery and a small brewery interested, although they weren't going there today, and the Jersey Gals cheese shop in the afternoon, before returning to Barrington. The group were chatting and asking questions and Lucas appeared really comfortable as their tour guide. Harry hoped he could do it half as well when it was his turn.

10

Finn

Finn served the wine tastings, but was happy to let Lucas do the talking. He was impressed when after a short explanation, his son deftly handed over to Harry, who although less knowledgeable about the wines was frank and funny and stayed on message.

'If you like it, then it's good.' Harry swirled the merlot in the bottom of his glass. 'I don't have to know if the grapes were picked by vestal virgins on the south side of the hill during a full moon. I hear my friend Lucas here talking about tannins, acidity and oak-influence, but really it's all just blah blah blah to me. I like it. I'll buy it. The label looks kinda upmarket, I'd happily bring it to the dinner. You know, the one where you're going to meet the girl's besties, or her parents, or maybe the new work colleagues.' The group was hanging off his words, smiling and chuckling and sipping their wine. Robbie looked especially chuffed.

They moved to the large outdoor tables for lunch, with the boys still chatting to their guests in a friendly, informal way. Hanna, bless her, served the salads and ensured everyone had enough to eat, including a tray of petite sweets. They were going to the cheese place on the way back to town and Lucas didn't want them to be too full.

Back in the tasting room, Finn was stacking glasses in the dishwasher as everyone was getting ready to leave. Judith appeared at the counter.

'Can I help you, Judith?' Finn smiled at the older woman, she'd fitted in with the younger ones today with no difficulty.

'I'd like to buy half a case of your wine, Finn. Three of the white, the sauvignon blanc and three of the merlot please.'

Finn blinked. Today was a test run for the boys. He hadn't expected to sell any wines. He was about to tell Judith this, when she leaned forward, whispering conspiratorially. 'I've been meaning to come out here to pick up some of your white wine. But tasting the merlot today was a bonus. I'm using today as an excuse. Don't judge me.' Judith laughed, then winked.

Laughing, Finn nodded. 'Well in that case Judith, I'll pack them up and bring them out to the vehicle.'

'Excellent. Ring it up, Finn. I'm planning to pick up an assortment of cheese at our next stop and I'll be set for tonight.' Judith laughed, credit card in hand.

When Finn walked the carton of wine out to the car, Lucas looked flustered as he approached. 'I'll drive and you jump in the back Harry.'

'Okay mate.' Harry agreed readily enough and Finn walked to the back of the vehicle with him, Judith's wine still in his arms. He saw Robbie hold the passenger door open to help Judith in.

Finn spoke quietly. 'Is Luke okay, Harry? He was fine ten minutes ago and now he looks, I don't know, out of sorts?' Finn wasn't sure if Harry would tell him, even if he knew.

Harry moved closer to Finn. 'Actually, Callum was just chatting with Meggie about his sister, Freddie, coming home to work at the Vet clinic. Kristen mentioned it a few nights ago when we were all together at the pub.' His mouth formed a grim line. 'I just hope she doesn't …'

Harry didn't have to finish that thought. Finn's mind was already racing. Freddie had broken Luke's heart. He'd hoped he was over her. *The heart wants what the heart wants.* His own words, spoken to Millie when they'd first begun seeing each other.

Finn shook his head as he handed the carton of bottles to Harry and patted him on the shoulder. 'Thanks mate. Better we know.'

'My thoughts too, Finn.'

As the vehicle pulled away, Finn waved, then walked back into the tasting room. Lucas was older now and he knew what Freddie was like...but still he sighed.

11

Samantha

'FIRST DAY OF LAST TERM AND EVIE CAME HOME ASKING about Christmas again.' Samantha handed Jamie the last big pot to dry.

'Christmas? Or Santa?' Jamie dried the pot, put it away and hung the wet cloth over the oven door. Samantha loved that he never minded helping with household chores. But then, she did a lot of farm work outdoors with him, too.

'We're a good team, Jamie Tait.' Samantha wrapped her arms around his waist. 'But it was Christmas she asked about. Specifically, she asked if I buy the presents. She was with me last year when we bought some small things.'

'So how did you answer?' Jamie kissed her forehead.

'I said yes, I do buy presents. Because it's nice to buy gifts for those we love. And Santa only brings one present for each little boy and girl.' Samantha nibbled her bottom lip.

'Good answer. How did she take it?' Jamie took her hand and they moved along the hallway quietly. He opened the door to Warwick's bedroom. He was fast asleep, one leg out of the covers and a toy horse in his hand.

Creeping into the room, Jamie tucked his son back in but was unable to pry the toy from his grip. Closing the door, they moved along the hall and opened Evie's door. She was snuggled so deeply in the bed that only the top of her head was visible. A ballerina doll wearing a tutu was on the floor by her bed. Jamie crept forward and picked it up, tucking it into bed beside her.

Turning the hall light out, they moved to their own room, continuing the conversation, but no longer needing to whisper.

'She frowned a little bit. You know how she does when she's working something out?' Samantha pulled her shirt over her head. 'Do you think I should say more?'

Jamie stood, watching her closely. *She knew that look.* 'No. Wait until she asks again. But I do think we should start planning for Christmas.'

'Planning?' She sat on the bed to pull her jeans off.

'Let me help you.' Jamie's tone changed as he stepped forward, brushing her tummy with his hands as he undid the top button of her jeans.

Planning. Tomorrow. Need to revisit that conversation. Samantha pulled Jamie down, kissing him soundly.

12

Evie (two months to Christmas)

'Is too! My brother says he is!' I stamped my foot at Cam Jennings and tried to peer around him. I needed Woz to back me up. Cam had me cornered near the vegetable garden, where I'd chased a tennis ball.

'Your brother? You don't have a brother, Evie Scott!' Cam Jennings picked up the tennis ball I'd been looking for, and threw it out the door.

'Do too! Woz is my brother!' I sniffed, trying to hold back my tears. *Where is Woz when I need him?*

'Santa isn't real, Warwick Tait isn't your brother and Jamie Tait isn't your father. Your mum isn't even married to Jamie, they're living in sin.' The way he said *sin* made me feel bad and sorta dirty. I remembered hearing about sin *before*. Before we lived in Barrington. When mummy was sad.

I rushed forward and shoved Cam Jennings as hard as I could, pushing him over on his bottom. I didn't care that I was crying now and I kicked his leg with the tip of my shoe as I ran past. 'You don't know anything about anything, Cam Jennings!' I heard him cry out, but I didn't care.

Still running, I turned the corner of the sports shed and flew straight into Woz, almost knocking him to the ground. He put one arm around me and asked me what was wrong but I didn't want to tell him. So all I said was, 'Cam Jennings. I pushed him over.'

'Evie Scott, can you please come to the office?' Miss Rogers was standing in front of the library with Cam Jennings beside her. Her voice was loud and a bit scary.

'No!' I shouted at her and stayed right where I was.

'She'll call Samantha, and Dad, and they'll have to come to school.' Woz held my hand and pulled me towards the teacher. 'Come on. You might have to say sorry to Cam.'

Dragging my feet, I followed Woz. I didn't want to look at Cam or say sorry to him. I wasn't sorry.

'What's this about, Evie? Cam said you pushed him over?' Miss Rogers spoke gently, which made me cry but I didn't want to repeat what Cam had said. Not in front of Woz.

'He was teasing her, Miss.' Woz stuck up for me.

'Were you there, Warwick Tait?' She sounded cross now.

'No Miss.' Woz didn't budge. 'But he teases her a lot.'

Miss Rogers changed direction then, so quickly that I stopped crying.

'Is that true, Cam? Do you tease Evie? I'd like you to remember that she is a prep student and you are in grade two. Older students have a duty of care to the younger students. I might have to speak to your father about your behaviour.' I saw Woz smirk out of the corner of my eye.

Cam Jennings shuffled his feet in the dirt, then looked directly at me. 'I was only joking Miss. Evie took it all wrong.'

Miss Rogers frowned at Cam. Hard. Then she looked at me, but Woz still had hold of my hand so I was brave and stared straight back at her. After a minute she told us to say sorry to each other.

I didn't want to, but Woz tugged on my hand after Cam mumbled, 'sorry Evie.' He didn't mean it. We all knew that. Well, maybe not Miss Rogers.

I smiled my biggest, brightest smile and said as sweetly as I could, 'thank you Cam.' Woz nudged me with his elbow. 'I'm sorry you got in the way and fell over when I was chasing the tennis ball.'

Cam Jennings glared at me. I smiled at him.

'Go and ring the bell, Cam. Lunchtime is over.' Miss Rogers gave me one more serious look before she disappeared into the library. Cam pointed a finger at me, but didn't say anything. He walked to the big kids classroom and rang the bell.

'What did Cam say to you?' Woz whispered to me as we walked back to our class.

'Tell you later.' But I won't tell him. I won't ever tell him that.

13

___

Freddie

Driving slowly away from Sterling Station, Freddie glanced in the rearview mirror to check the horse trailer she was towing for the third time, before focussing again on the road ahead. She was leaving three days earlier than planned, delivering two mares to a horse stud near Scone on the way home, for her boss, Bart Sterling Senior. She'd leave the horse trailer there and he'd send one of the station hands for it in a few weeks.

Freddie wasn't sure if her boss knew she had been fooling around with his son. But if he did, he must blame Bart Junior for it as he couldn't have been nicer to Freddie. He even gave her an unexpected bonus with her final pay. He said it was for the horse delivery, but she suspected it was more than that. A pleasant way of telling her that while he didn't blame her for his son's behaviour, he didn't want her back at Sterling Station any time soon.

Bart and Victoria had announced their engagement ten days ago and Freddie had heard Victoria whining about her.

'Why is that red-headed tart still here, Bartholemew?' Victoria had snarled the words at that first barbecue, loud enough for half the station hands to hear. Freddie wasn't sure how she knew about the affair, if you could call it that. But for the next two weeks Victoria was never far from Bart and kept a close watch on Freddie.

Freddie chuckled. Victoria had done her a favour. Not that she would ever tell her that. She'd seen Bart Sterling in a whole new light. Arrogant and confident when his father wasn't around, he appeared smaller and younger when the boss was home. And with Victoria, well, it was easy to see that she was made of steely stuff, and despite her petite and cultured exterior, Freddie suspected she had more balls than her fiancée. Or maybe more power in the relationship. Or perhaps her family had more money and more power. *Whatever.*

Freddie shrugged. She would have tired of Bart sooner or later. She knew now she'd fallen for the person he pretended to be, not the person he actually was, and she was driving home with no regrets. *Except for Lucas.* She regretted him. Not a minute of being with him, but for being too young and arrogant and stupid to realise he was a better man than most she'd known. Despite their different backgrounds, and bank accounts, Lucas was a better man than Bartholemew Sterling. He had walked away from her, from her games, even though he loved her. *Lucas Anderson has principles.*

Sighing, Freddie turned onto the highway carefully, checking again that the horse trailer was riding properly behind her old Landcruiser. And that was how she knew she'd never have another chance with Luke. She'd blown it. She'd apologised at the time, and he'd accepted her apology with grace. But he'd never trust her again. Shaking her head, Freddie wiped a lone tear that streaked down her cheek. What was that old saying? *The one you miss is the one you'll never have?*

14

———————

Hannelore

'Are you sure you don't want to come to the Chamber meeting tonight, Mum?' Hanna looked up as she counted the day's takings. 'We're down again on this time last year, but up a bit on last week.'

Millie peered at the number on Hanna's phone. 'Not as bad as it could be. We'll be okay.' She straightened. 'No, now that you've started going to the meetings, I don't feel the need.' Millie turned the sign to closed on the front door. 'And Finn is the same. You and Luke tell us anything we need to know, plus we get the meeting minutes.'

'But you'd come if we needed you to, wouldn't you?' Hanna sent the takings through to the bank electronically and turned the machine off.

Millie paused as she reached for the lasagne she was taking out to Finn's place. 'Of course. Is there something you need me to be there for?'

'You know we've been tossing around ideas, via emails mostly, about how we can use the drought relief funding? Hanna leaned back and called out. 'You almost ready, Kristen? We need to be there in twenty.' Kristen gave her a thumbs up and Hanna turned her attention back to Millie, who said something Hanna missed.

'Sorry Mum, start again please.' Hanna chuckled as Millie rolled her eyes.

'Yes. I spoke about this with Ben Evans a few days go. The funding is from State government, but it's administered by local Council.' Millie perched on a high stool behind the counter. Hanna noticed she didn't seem to be struggling with hot flashes today. Is she over it? Is it that quick? Or is she taking something to ease the symptoms?

'And therein lies the problem. Chamber members wanted to just split the funding, distributing a little bit to every member. But that became tricky as not every local business is a member, so Council said no to that. And to be honest, a few hundred dollars won't help people like Merv stay open longer hours.' Hanna moved closer to the counter to make room for Kristen.

'Council wants us, as a Chamber, to use the money for promotion. That way all businesses may benefit, to some extent.' Kristen patted Hanna on the shoulder. 'And Hanna has an idea, but we need it to go through at the meeting.'

Hanna nodded to Kristen and continued. 'It's not a big thing. But I'm going to suggest a competition, for the main street busi-nesses, to do up their shopfront window displays for Christmas.' The words tumbled out and Hanna felt herself flush, but kept going. 'But I wasn't sure I'd get any enthusiasm, until I spoke with Rose.'

'With Ben?' Millie looked confused. 'As a member of local Council?'

'Yes! You're quick Mum.' Hanna took a breath. 'Council would contribute a small amount to every business that participates in the window competition, but that in itself may not get them going. And now, here's the icing on the cake.' Hanna paused, she had their attention. *Good, because this is what she needs to do in the meeting tonight.* 'There will be ten thousand dollars in total prize money from Council for the best three displays, but that's not all.'

'It isn't?' Kristen wrinkled her nose. Hanna hadn't told her the best bit yet.

'They have a further thirty thousand dollars for pre-Christmas out-of-region promotion. And Ben believes it could be used to promote the main street displays and hold a special Christmas Night Market with music, local produce, Santa for the kids and announce the competition winners.' Hanna took a breath. 'But only if Chamber members are on board. We need more thought around the promotional spend. And quickly if it is to go ahead. It's already October and I'd like the window displays to be completed by mid-November, so we can market to visitors to come and have a look.'

Millie and Kristen still looked unsure. Hanna pushed on. 'Do you remember when Matty and I were little, Mum, and you and Dad would drive us around after dinner to see all the Christmas lights? There were a few streets that really got on board, almost like a competition to outdo each other. Every single house was lit up and I heard later they had a street party one night each year that everyone in the street came to.'

'Oh.' Millie's expression lightened. 'So that's the look and feel you're going for? Turn main street Barrington into a Christmas street party, with window displays and lights, and on one night a party and night market.' Millie's eyes were shining and Hanna felt her chest puff up with pride.

'And if we do it right Mum, and start in November, we have a good chance we can turn it into something that will bring people here for a look, and experience the street party atmosphere, just like we did when we were little.' Hanna waited, looking from Millie to Kristen.

'Wow! It's great Hanna. You already have my vote and Luke will have Finn's.' Millie checked her watch, then stood up. 'Is Harry going?'

'Yes.' Hanna bounced on her toes. 'So, he can vote on behalf of Wine for Blokes. They don't have a window to do up but I'm sure they can do something with their vehicle.'

'It really doesn't matter.' Millie picked up the covered tray containing the lasagne. 'The point is, even if Finn and I go, you already have the votes from our businesses.' She kissed Hanna on the cheek. 'You've got this, my clever girl.'

15

Harry

As Hanna spoke to her idea at the Chamber of Commerce meeting, Harry's mind was racing. He'd been wondering how Wine for Blokes could be part of the competition and promotion, without a shop front to decorate. It came to him as Hanna referenced the way they used to drive around to see the Christmas lights when she was a kid.

'That's it!' He didn't mean to speak aloud, but the words came out at the exact moment Hanna opened her motion up for discussion.

'Harry?' Chamber President, Meggie Hamilton-Masters nodded to him front the front table. 'Would you like to start the discussion?'

Grimacing, Harry shook his head. 'Er, no, thank you Meggie. I'm sure others, with, er, more experience should go first.'

'Alright Harry, but I will come back to you.' Meggie smiled

and Harry felt encouraged. He was keen to hear if anyone else had the same idea.

Merv from the bakery raised his hand.

'Go ahead, Merv.' Meggie held up a hand as two others began speaking at the same time. 'Members. Merv has the floor.'

'It's not a lot of funding, even for those who win the competition. I'm not convinced that people from the city would come all the way to Barrington to see our main street Christmas display. And the night market idea is good, but it's just one night.' Merv glanced at Hanna. Harry could see she was nervous, and excited too. He really wanted this to work for her. 'But well done Hanna, it's still the best idea we've had.' Merv smiled at Hanna and she visibly relaxed.

'It's a stupid idea. No one will come here for this. My shop is in a side street and it'll cost me to decorate.' Trev glared at Meggie, who merely thanked him for his opinion. Harry could see Kristen tapping away on her laptop, noting the comments.

Ben Evans cleared his throat. 'It has merit. And it does create another reason for people to visit. The evening event closer to Christmas will certainly draw visitors, and locals, together.' He paused and Harry could see how Ben managed to get the attention of the room without raising his voice. *Clever. A skill that could be learned.* 'But Merv, and Trev, if it has any chance at all we need to be on message. Not just the Chamber members, but all retailers. And Council.' Turning, he addressed Trev directly. 'Council is aware that some businesses may not have funds set aside to spend on decorations, so if everyone agrees, a small stipend will be provided to all businesses for this purpose. The funds will be drawn back if any business does not participate as arranged.'

That seemed to take the wind out of Trev's sails and he settled, scribbling some notes on the agenda in front of him. *Good. He's making plans now.*

The discussion continued and the group appeared to be taking on board the opportunity. No one else had mentioned the idea that had come to Harry, and he wondered if he should bring it up, or speak to Hanna first, afterwards, in case it was a stupid idea. They were discussing themes now. Christmas, obviously, but whether they should try to co-ordinate colours.

As if reading his mind, Meggie called on him. 'Harry, you had an idea as we started this discussion. Would you like to share it?'

Tensing a bit, Harry clenched one hand under the table, but relaxed somewhat when Hanna's smaller hand crept into his. *Here goes.* 'I think Hanna's idea is great, but what if we dig deeper?' He caught the look of surprise on her face, but she nodded encouragingly. 'I don't have any marketing skills Meggie, but when Hanna talked about how they used to drive around the streets to see the Christmas lights when she was young, it brought up a memory for me.' He patted his chest. 'And a really strong feeling.' He tried to keep his voice low and modulated, like Ben did, but he allowed some excitement to slip in because he really thought he was on to something.

Looking around the room, he spoke quietly. 'Who else did this? Drove around to see the lights when you were a kid? Or perhaps took your own children out in the car after dinner to see Christmas lights?'

Everyone was smiling at him now, and several spoke at once about their experiences. He could see Meggie watching him closely, but she made no move to stop the discussion.

'And can I ask you now, all of you, how do you feel? Right now? Remembering that experience? Your own, or the excitement on your children's faces?' Harry leaned forward. All of their expressions had changed. Some looked nostalgic, some laughing with the person next to them. All of them were smiling, even Trev.

'We didn't have much when we were kids. Life was tough for us.' Trev spoke first and the room quietened. 'I always wanted more for my kids. But we had them young, and didn't have much money.' He chuckled. 'Four kids under six when we opened our first shop in Hornsby. We lived upstairs and Marge helped during the day and did the bookwork at night.'

Trev shook his head, but his face seemed softer. 'Sometimes I'd take the youngest one for a drive in the car, to get her to sleep. Marge had her hands full getting the other three to bed.' He looked directly at Harry, and continued. 'One night, close to Christmas, I drove down one street and saw almost all the houses in two full blocks had decorated for Christmas, some with a tree lit up in their front window with lights on it. One had a sleigh and reindeer on his roof.' He chuckled. 'No idea how they got them up there.'

Trev drew in a sharp breath and Harry could see he was really moved. He was about to speak, but Trev continued. 'So the next night, we all went. The baby slept through it, of course, but the others were excited to stay up a bit later. They already had their pyjamas on when we got in the car and we told them we were going to show them some Christmas magic.' Trev nodded at Hanna. 'I haven't thought about that for a long time, but we did it for several years, until we moved here, actually. And they all remember it, often mentioning it when we're together for Christmas. Hanna, I want to apologise, I think this is a fabulous idea.'

'Thank you, Trev.' Harry grinned. 'Your experience, I think, raises memories for many of us.' He smiled at Hanna, then looked around the room. 'I don't think we're selling a *Christmas lights experience* or a *night market event*. I think we're selling *Christmas magic, Barrington Magic*.' He nodded to Trev who seemed chuffed. 'If we do it right, market it properly, it will bring people here to recreate a version of their own memories, and create new ones with their families.'

Hanna was beaming and Harry thought he must be grinning like a loon. But he wasn't finished. 'I have another question for you Trev, if you don't mind?'

'Go ahead Harry.' Trev looked soft, and sort of vulnerable, so Harry paused while he put his thoughts together.

'Your kids, and their kids. Will they come this year for Christmas with you and Marge?'

'Some will. It's been a long time since they all came. The youngest one says she won't come until New Year. Why?' Trev seemed confused.

'Tell them to come this year, Trev. Tell them about *Barrington Magic*. If it brings up fond memories for them, as it has with you, I think they'll all come. They can make some *Christmas magic* memories with you and their own children.' Harry leaned back, suddenly aware the room was silent and all eyes were on him.

Merv began to clap. A slow clap like they do at the footy when they win. Lucas started clapping too, and Kristen and Meggie and suddenly the whole room erupted into something loud and positive and happy.

Harry grinned, then held up his hand for them to stop, imitating the way Meggie ran the meeting. 'And I haven't discussed this with my business partner yet, but Wine for Blokes could offer Barrington Magic night tours. For those travelling by train, and maybe for family groups that want to be together in one vehicle.'

'Your partner is on board.' Lucas laughed out loud. 'I think we could package that up nicely.'

Meggie waved, returning the attention of the group to the front of the room. 'Harry Stewart, you've taken a great idea and made it brilliant. I love *Christmas Magic, Barrington Magic* as a theme and a perfect name for the program and event. What do you think Hanna?'

'Oh, I've known for a long time that there's more to Harry Stewart. He's not just a pretty face.' Hanna giggled, Harry blushed and in just a few minutes the meeting was over.

'Staying for some pizza, Luke?' Harry nudged his pal on the shoulder.

'Sure. Aren't you the man of the moment?' Lucas nudged him back.

Kristen joined them. 'Can we grab a larger booth? Callum messaged that he's coming into town.'

Hanna almost skipped into the main dining room, slipping into a large booth. She snapped her fingers. 'Prosecco please Harry, we're celebrating.'

THREE PIZZAS AND TWO BOTTLES OF PROSECCO LATER, Harry kept an eye on Hanna. She was tipsy, and so was Kristen. Callum was driving Kristen home and Harry would walk Hanna to her place and stay the night. Millie was out at Finn's. In fact, she seemed to stay out there a lot and Harry wondered if she would end up living at the winery with Finn in the future. They were a lovely couple.

Harry had plans of his own with Hanna. He just hadn't decided when.

They were getting ready to leave when Callum waved his phone about. 'Oh, hold on Kristen. Freddie is just a few minutes away, she's going to meet us here.'

'Freddie?' Harry stood up, Lucas was at the bar getting another drink. 'I thought she was due home at the weekend?'

'Yeah. She's ahead of schedule. She delivered a couple of mares to a place over past Scone for her old boss, but she decided to push on to Barrington instead of staying overnight.' He turned to Kristen. 'I'll see if I can order something for her, she'll be hungry.'

'The kitchen will be closed, Cal.' But he ignored Harry and strode to the bar. Harry and Hanna exchanged a glance as Callum spoke briefly with Lucas.

Beer in hand, Lucas walked back to them. 'Can I stay at yours tonight, Hanna?' He held the beer up. 'I'm over the limit to drive home.'

'Of course.' Hanna smiled at Lucas and put her arm through his. 'Drink that one and come over with Harry, when you're ready.'

Lucas drank the whole beer down as if it was nothing and placed the empty glass on the table. 'Let's go then. I'm ready. You got anything sweet over there for dessert?'

Harry walked out with them. *Oh, yeah. Lucas still has feelings for Freddie Campbell.*

16

Finn

'I'M WORRIED ABOUT LUKE.' FINN PUSHED THE FRUIT platter closer to Millie. 'I had hoped he was over Freddie Campbell, but in the few days she's been back he's barely left the property.'

'It's almost two years since she left.' Millie piled fruit onto her plate and topped it up with natural yoghurt. 'She came into the café this week, she's working at the Vet Clinic two days a week.'

'How was she?' Finn pushed the fruit around in his plate.

'Honestly?' Millie raised an eyebrow. 'Different. Perhaps more grown up. I'm not sure. But she was friendly and polite.'

'She was always friendly and polite, Millie. She had us all fooled. That wholesome country-girl exterior hid a shameless lack of concern for others. Lucas in particular.' Finn shook his head. 'I'm unsure if she's changed, or matured as you suggest. Maybe she's just got better at hiding her true colours.'

'I know you're worried about Luke, but Finn, he's matured too. And his business with Harry is going well plus he's taken on more responsibility here.' Millie placed her hand over his. 'He's a grown man and you need to trust his decisions. It seems, at the moment, that he's avoiding Freddie. But if she stays here, he'll have to work out how to deal with her, socially, at least.'

'You're right. I know you're right.' Finn stared at his plate. 'Would you like some honey to drizzle over that, Millie?'

'Mmmm. Yes please!' The way she said it made him laugh and reach for the honey.

'You're making honey sound kinda naughty, Millie.' Finn chuckled deeply. 'Be careful what you wish for.'

'Actually, I'm feeling so much better lately, since I got onto those natural supplements to help my menopause symptoms.' She winked at him and he laughed again.

'Stop it! There's no time for shenanigans this morning. I'm setting up for the small wedding event here tomorrow.' Finn leaned over and kissed Millie soundly on the lips. 'You can take that,' he kissed her again, 'to work with you today.'

They finished breakfast quickly and he washed up while Millie got her stuff together to head back into town. When she reappeared she looked fresh and gorgeous and he wished they had no commitments to rush off to.

'Are you coming back here tonight, Millie? I can throw a steak on the barbecue and there's still salad left from last night.' *Did he sound desperate? Or just hopeful?*

'That would be four nights in a row, Finn Anderson. I'm in danger of overstaying my welcome.' Her eyes twinkled and Finn walked over and wrapped his arms around her.

'You could never overstay your welcome with me, Millie. I'd

have you here every night.' He felt her body tense as he said it and he chastised himself silently. *They'd talked about this. She wants to keep her independence. Keep her own place.*

Millie took a half step back and Finn was preparing to water down his words, make light of them. But when he looked into her face she wasn't upset by what he'd said, at all. She had a tiny smile curling up the edges of her lips. *Such kissable lips.* Almost drawling, she countered with, 'be careful what *you* wish for, Finn.'

Really? A bubble of hope exploded in his chest. 'This may not be the right time Millie, but are you suggesting you might like to stay here more often? Because I can make that happen.'

Millie turned, picked up her things and walked toward the door. Actually, she didn't walk, she sashayed, swaying her hips from side to side. It was all he could do not to laugh, it was so unexpected. But then she stopped and shot him a smouldering look over her shoulder. 'I'm coming back tonight, Finn. Ask me then, how often I'd like to stay here.'

And she was gone. Finn sat for a moment at the kitchen table. *Ask her?* He was pretty sure she didn't want to remarry, they'd talked about that a lot, although he would in a heartbeat. But asking her to move in, to live with him, didn't feel right either. Millie Tucker had given him something to think about, that was for sure.

17

Samantha

THE MORNING WAS CHAOTIC, AS USUAL. WARWICK couldn't find his sports shoes, then Evie remembered he'd left them up at the big house, so they had to race up there before catching the bus. Jill had wanted to chat about the Christmas promotion in town and Evie had let BlueDog jump up on her, leaving muddy footprints on her school shirt. Jill sponged them out and as they ran out to the car, the school bus trundled by.

Samantha bundled the kids into the car and raced down the road to follow the bus, so they could get on at the next stop.

It wasn't until she got back to their cottage that Samantha realised she hadn't eaten breakfast. Popping a slice of bread in the toaster, she peered out through the window hoping to catch a glimpse of Jamie, as he usually came in for a cup of tea around this time.

The sound of the motorbike and a dog barking told her Jamie

was back and she poured hot water into the teapot. He strode in, all smiles, kissed her gently then pulled their cups from the cupboard.

'Want some toast, Jamie? I didn't get a chance earlier.' Samantha placed two plates on the table, along with the condiments, before he answered.

'Why not?' When it was ready he brought the toast across from the counter and put a piece on her plate, then his. He passed her the butter, but she hesitated, her knife hovering over the butter dish. Pushing it towards Jamie, she reached for the peanut butter instead.

'Peanut butter? Really Sam? I thought you hated peanut butter?' Jamie slathered his own toast with butter and Vegemite.

'Funny isn't it, how a food you've never liked, suddenly appeals?' She was about to say more, but something caused her stomach to roll. The smell of the tea perhaps? Springing from her chair Samantha rushed to the bathroom and retched into the toilet bowl. She stayed on her haunches for a moment, then stood, feeling a little shaky.

Jamie appeared in the doorway. 'Sam?'

Waving him away, she muttered. 'I'm okay. Might just be a stomach bug.'

'Could be.' Jamie folded his arms cross his chest. 'But Sam, could it be something else?'

The colour left her face as she perched on the edge of the bathtub. Looking up at him, she tried to concentrate, and count back. *Could she be pregnant?*

Jamie sat beside her and took her hands in his. 'We've talked about this Sam. That one day we might have a child together.' He chuckled. 'I think it might be *one day* already.'

'You're not upset? It's sooner than we'd talked about.' Samantha felt anxious suddenly. Everything had been going so well for them, she wasn't sure if they were ready for this.

'First things first.' Jamie stood up and held out his hand for her. 'It might be a tummy bug. Best to check before we get too excited.'

'Excited? Will you be excited Jamie? If it is. You know.' Samantha couldn't say it aloud.

Scooping her up in his arms, Jamie carried her back to the kitchen and sat her gently on her chair. 'Absolutely Sam. We're ready for this.' He took the toast away. 'Let's start over. You need to eat something. What appeals?'

18

Evie (six weeks to Christmas)

Miss Rogers helped us start a letter to Santa in class today. I didn't even know we could do that. I thought Santa just watched, all year, and brought you something you'd like.

Everyone else started their Santa letters, but I didn't. I told Miss Rogers I need to think about it. We had a special piece of paper to write on, with bits to colour in around the edges. So I just coloured mine in.

The other thing that bothers me is that I can't write many words yet. Miss Rogers put some words on the board that we could copy, and then she came around to help everyone with their letter. But I want my letter to be private, just for Santa. I slipped it into my bag and brought it home.

I've been thinking about what I want to ask Santa for, and Mummy told me a long time ago that it's just one thing from Santa. I have an idea, but I need help to write it.

After school we rode on the quad bike with Jamie to check on the springers. That's cows who are ready to have a baby calf. When the calf comes, Jamie moves the mother and baby into a paddock close to our house.

I asked Woz what he asked Santa for. He finished his letter in class and Miss Rogers sealed it up and put it in a special red box. She's going to post them to Santa on the weekend. Woz said he asked for a motorbike, a small one especially for kids. I'd like one of those too, but I have something more important in mind.

We helped move two cows and calves to the house paddock, then Jamie said he was taking us to the big house for afternoon tea, because Mummy was running errands in town. I wondered if I should ask Jamie to help me write my letter.

We sat up at the table and had chocolate milk and a lamington each.

'How was school today, young Evie?' Pa always asks me about school. 'What was the best thing you did today?'

Woz jumped in then. 'We wrote our letters to Santa. Wanna know what I asked for?'

'I do not, young man.' Pa's voice sounded stern, but he never really gets cross. He has big bushy black eyebrows and sometimes they move up and down when he talks. 'That's between you and Santa.'

'And did you also write a letter to Santa today, Evie?' His eyebrows came together when I said no.

'Evie was slow. But she has the letter, she just needs to finish it and give it to Miss Rogers on Friday.' Woz reached for another lamington but Jamie moved the plate away. 'Ohh, Daa-ad.'

Jamie stood up quickly. 'Say thank you to Nanna, we'd better head home.' I wondered why he was in a hurry. I sat on the back step to put my shoes back on. Nanna walked out to the clothesline and Jamie said he'd help her. Woz ran out into the yard, throwing an old ball for the dogs.

Pa sat down beside me and asked if I needed help with my shoelaces, but I've gotten really good at doing them up now. But he asked so kindly, I looked at him for a moment and then I whispered to him that there was something he could help me with.

He looked surprised when I explained, but he said he was happy to help. 'Do you have it with you Evie?'

I shook my head. 'My bag is at the house.'

We stared at each other. He seemed to get an idea then. 'Come over here before school tomorrow morning. Tell Mummy you forgot something. We can do it then.'

'Okay Pa.' I jumped up and hugged his neck tightly.

He laughed loudly. 'Off you go, Evie.' Leaning closer, he whispered, 'I'll see you in the morning.'

I WAS UP VERY EARLY AND RAN ACROSS THE PADDOCK TO the big house with my gumboots on and my half-finished letter folded carefully in my hand and a pencil in my pocket. Opening the back door, I could hear the kettle whistling and knew Nanna and Pa would be sitting at the table together.

I kicked my boots off at the door and ran inside in my socks. Nanna looked surprised to see me, but not Pa.

'Would you like a hot chocolate Evie, or some orange juice?' Nanna bustled over to the fridge while I pulled my chair close to Pa.

'Orange juice please Nanna.' I slid the letter closer to him. 'This is our secret Pa, no one else must know.'

Nanna brought the juice to me and glanced at the letter, still folded in half. I put my hand over it. She said she had to do something in the laundry and walked away.

I unfolded the letter and smoothed it out as best as I could. It was a bit crumpled.

Pa pointed to the bits I'd coloured in. 'Did it come like this Evie?'

I giggled and shook my head. 'No, I coloured it all in myself.'

'Very nice.'

All I had written at school was ..

Dear Santa

'What would you like to say Evie, and I'll help you spell the words, but you can write them.'

I took a big breath, then I whispered it to him. He didn't say anything at all for a moment, but then he turned the paper towards me.

'I think we keep it simple Evie, so Santa doesn't get confused.'

We worked together for a little while. Nanna came in once but I covered the letter with my hands and she left again. When it was done, Pa read it quietly to me one more time, and then I signed it.

Evie Scott

'Alright young Evie, how about I drive you home, it must be breakfast time at your place.' Pa held my hand and helped me climb in his old ute, then we bumped our way around the track to our house.

I thanked him with a kiss on the cheek and he laughed and said he wouldn't wash his face all day, which made me laugh too.

19

———

Freddie

'Would you like to decorate the Clinic window for Christmas?' Angus grinned at Freddie. 'You know Max and I will stuff it up, and Melanie says she can help, if you'll take it on.'

'What's the theme? Everyone's been talking about it on social media. It's a competition, isn't it?' Freddie was keen. She'd been getting two clinic days a week and one big animal day, and if rain came soon, business would pick up and she'd have full time work with Barrington Vets.

'Yep. The theme is *Christmas Magic, Barrington Magic* to bring visitors and locals to see the decorations along the main street in the weeks leading up to Christmas. There's a Night Market event on just before Christmas to announce the winners.' Angus moved closer to their window.

It was a bay window and Freddie stepped right into it. They changed their display monthly and it was currently full of information on protecting your animals from ticks. To one side was a bale of hay topped with a pyramid of dog food cans they recommended for young animals. General information covered the back wall of the window, so it was enclosed and people outside the shop couldn't see who was in the waiting room.

Melanie appeared and poked her head in. 'It's a bit uninspiring Freddie. Any ideas? We've got a lot of tinsel and baubles and some Santa hats.' She glanced at Angus. 'I can raid petty cash if you need anything in particular.'

'Let me think about it. When do we need to have it done?' Freddie held out her arms to measure the space. An idea was forming.

'This Friday.' Max appeared now, holding a cup of coffee. 'Meggie says the early promo is gathering interest, and they have a local photographer booked this weekend to take pictures of all the displays.

The front door opened and an older woman walked in carrying a cat cage. Angus leapt forward to hold the door open. 'Mrs Tubbs, you're right on time and the first one in. Come through to the surgery and I'll check Ginge over and give him his shots.'

Freddie followed Melanie back to reception, as two more owners and patients walked in. 'Quick question Melanie?'

'Yes?' Melanie was tapping her keyboard, but stopped and gazed at Freddie.

'We used to get posters from some of the suppliers. There were a few, quite big ones, of gorgeous border collies with shiny coats. Do we still have those?' Freddie leaned forward, watching as Max chatted to a young boy in the waiting room with a small dog.

'Oh yes.' Melanie rolled her eyes. 'Angus never throws

anything out. They should be in that big cupboard in the animal hospital. There's a lot of stuff in there, some of it may be useful.'

But it was after lunch when Freddie finally delved into the storage cabinet. She found several large posters of the collie dog – jumping to catch a Frisbee, riding on the back of a quad bike with its tongue lolling, running over the backs of a mob of sheep and another laying by a fire with two little kids patting it. There were a few other posters, some of cows and horses. Freddie giggled. She had some fun ideas and hoped Angus and Max would approve.

Melanie called her back to reception mid-afternoon. 'Can you cover reception until closing please Freddie? I'm picking Tiff up from school, then taking her to rehearsal at the hall.'

'Rehearsal?' Freddie slipped into the chair Melanie had vacated.

'The kids from the primary school are putting on a concert at the Night Market. They're all super excited!' Melanie picked up her purse and keys and dashed out through the back. 'See ya Freddie!'

Freddie walked to the pub after work. She was meeting Callum and Kristen for dinner. Kristen had said Hanna and Harry might be there too, which made Freddie nervous. But she'd already decided the best way forward, from now on, was with integrity. She'd apologise to Harry if she found the right moment.

20

Hannelore

Arriving late to the pub, Hanna had to squeeze in beside Harry, with Freddie on his other side. 'Hi everyone.' She smiled at Callum and Kristen and kissed Harry quickly then looked around him to greet Freddie. 'Nice to have you home Freddie, how are you settling in?'

'Hi Hanna. Yeah, good. Thank you.' Freddie passed her a menu. 'We've ordered some pizzas already, but is there something you'd like?

Laughing, Hanna set the menu aside. 'I'll have what you're having.' She touched the glass of wine in front of her and Harry nodded. She picked it up and sipped. *Sav Blanc. Excellent.*

Kristen giggled and Harry laughed out loud. He patted her leg. 'Funny girl.'

'Actually, I have some questions and I hope you and Kristen can help me, Hanna?' Freddie paused. 'About the Barrington

Magic competition and promotion. I'm doing the Vet Clinic window and I want to make sure I'm on theme.'

'Oh good!' Hanna was thrilled to hear Freddie taking it seriously too. 'Actually, it's grown out of proportion. Ridiculously so.' She nudged Harry. 'But in a good way.'

'Oh, tell me more.' Freddie leaned forward just as three pizzas were delivered to the table.

Hanna waited until everyone had wrestled a piece on to their plate. 'The latest development is quite short notice. All windows need to be finished by Friday evening for the photo shoot to create content for the promo. So then a whole discussion was had around the content.'

'Content?' Freddie mumbled, reaching for a serviette.

'Not just photos, but videos and reels for social media.' Hanna took a quick sip of wine. 'And now the local television station is coming because *Barrington Magic* is a *thing*!'

Kristen jumped in. 'Because all the main street businesses are participating, and we're going for that nostalgic family Christmas feel, now a whole bunch of houses in town are also decorating.'

'Not just houses. Whole streets are coordinating their efforts and they're planning to have old-fashioned Christmas street parties too.' Harry grinned. 'That was my idea, but hey, everyone is just running with it.'

'So to get the footage we need for promo, we're doing a soft launch this weekend. With a street party here in main street plus lots of streets in town for visitors to tour around.' Hanna tried to look innocent. 'Word is out and I think we'll have a lot of people coming in from the farms in the district too.'

'Council is running a sausage sizzle in the street on Saturday night and all of the food operators, like the cafe and the bakery and the butcher and so on, can run a market stall outside our shops, to create the feel of the Night Market for the promo ... you know, to create the content.' Hanna ran out of steam then, but was thrilled to see Freddie so engaged.

'Wow! I love it. Well done to you Hanna, and Harry and the Chamber of Commerce.' Freddie's eyes were shining and Hanna knew, in that instant, that she had changed. Maybe not changed, but grown up.

Hanna's suspicions were confirmed later, when Callum went to pay for more drinks and Kirsten dashed off to the bathroom.

Freddie turned to them. 'Harry, I want to apologise to you.' She smiled tentatively at Hanna. 'And this includes you too, Hanna. I behaved badly when I was home last time. I've only just realised how stupid and immature I was.' She shook her head sadly. 'I am truly sorry. I don't expect you to forgive me, or forget what I did. But you're friends with Kristen and Callum.' She grinned suddenly. 'And they are just so cute together! I don't want it to be awkward, for them or for you. But he's my favourite brother and I need to be there, you know, in his stuff.' She shuffled in her seat a bit.

Hanna wasn't sure what Harry thought, but she was all for forgive and forget. 'Freddie, thank you. Just hearing you say that warms my heart. I made some mistakes too, before I came here. I treated my Mum badly when I was younger and I know how it feels when you realise what you've done, or who you've hurt.' Hanna nudged Harry. 'So girlfriend, you hang around and get in your brother's stuff as much as you need to.'

Harry put an arm around Hanna and leaned back, gazing at Freddie. 'You're okay, Freddie Campbell. I always knew you would be. No hard feelings here.'

21

Finn

WHEN MILLIE ARRIVED AFTER WORK THE NEXT NIGHT, Finn hugged her tightly. 'Glass of wine Millie?'

'Hello you. Yes, wine would be lovely.' Millie kissed him quickly on the lips then plonked down in her favourite spot on the sofa as Finn strolled to the kitchen. 'Can I help with anything? I can freshen up that salad from last night.'

'No need. Everything is sorted.' With a glass of wine in each hand, Finn joined her on the sofa. 'Here you go, how was work today?'

'Busy. Hanna and Kristen are distracted by the window dressing competition and this "soft launch" event on Saturday night.' Millie sipped her wine and closed her eyes briefly. 'Ah, this is the ticket.'

'We've been roped in for Saturday night too. Lucas and Harry are going to use their vehicle as a sort-of impromptu wine cellar at the street party. They're combining Wine for Blokes with Barrington Estate Wines and doing some casual tastings.' Finn glanced at Millie. She seemed relaxed. 'They're using it as a bit of a promo for their business. I think they're hoping to be in the television footage.'

Millie chuckled. 'That might attract a lot more punters.' She sipped the last of her wine and held the empty glass up, looking surprised. 'I drank that a bit fast.'

'I've set up our dinner over at the tasting room, it's easier to throw a steak on over there. Salad and dessert are over there too.' Finn stood up, taking the glass from Millie. 'I'll leave these here, let's walk over now.'

'Okay.' Millie held out her hand for Finn to pull her to her feet. 'Is Luke here? Joining us?'

'He is. I hope you don't mind. But Hanna and Harry are here too. They wanted to have a get together about the promotion, window decorations and so on and Luke said they were sick of having pizza at the pub.' Finn held her hand as they strolled across.

'Honestly? I love being around the kids. I think they keep us young.' Millie walked through the door first and waved to Hanna setting the table. Harry and Luke were behind the bar, deep in conversation but they paused to greet her warmly.

Lucas took over the barbecue and Finn found himself sitting with Millie, enjoying the chatter and free flowing promotion ideas as the young ones prepared their meal.

Seated at the table, the easy banter continued as they passed bowls of salad and crusty dinner rolls to each other, as Lucas served them each a steak.

Leaning back, his meal finished, Finn slung an arm over the back of Millie's chair. Harry was cleaning the barbecue and Hanna began clearing their plates. 'Hold on a moment please Hanna.' Finn smiled at her. *So like her mother. Smart, business-like and very loving.* Finn looked at Luke, who cocked an eyebrow. 'You stay too, mate.'

'Harry, Dad needs us!' Lucas called out and Harry bounded over.

Finn had a moment of doubt, but having Harry hear what he wanted to say wouldn't make a spot of difference. Millie was looking at him curiously, but she was relaxed. He turned to her, taking her hands in his. 'Millie, we started a conversation in my kitchen yesterday morning, that I'd like to finish.'

Millie blinked. He could see she was searching her memory bank for exactly which conversation he meant. Then it dawned on her. She looked amused, rather than concerned, so he pushed on.

To the three young people, he explained. 'We've been spending a lot of time together.' He spoke directly to Hanna, 'and every night your Mum isn't here, I wish she was.' Millie giggled and nodded.

'Luke, hand me that guitar.' It was leaning against a chair near the door. He'd left it there earlier and Luke had asked him about it.

Picking up the guitar, Finn moved his chair back slightly, while he gazed at Millie. 'In front of witnesses, I want to tell you I've been learning a new song. Can I sing it to you?'

Millie was flushed and Finn wasn't sure if it was menopause, the wine or excitement. She nodded for him to go on. Finn strummed a few bars, then quietly sang All of Me. He almost stopped when Millie started to cry, and he smiled broadly when Hanna moved onto Harry's lap, her eyes misty.

At the end of the song Luke took the guitar from his hand and slapped him on the back, while Millie leaned forward and kissed him soundly on the mouth, while wiping her tears away. She whispered, 'that was beautiful Finn.'

'Is that all you're going to say, Mum?' Hanna glared at Millie for a moment. 'I think Finn just proposed to you!'

Millie nodded. 'I know, Hanna.' She gazed into his eyes and he found his own throat closing up. 'I've never felt more loved than I do right now, Finn Anderson.' Millie took his hand. 'And I know you were proposing *something*. But Finn, I don't know if I want to get married again.'

'Mum!' Hanna almost shouted, but Finn gave her a look and she settled.

'Millie, I'd marry you tomorrow, if that's what you want. But we've talked about it and I know it's not on your radar. Not yet anyway.' He couldn't look at Hanna, even though she drew in a loud breath. 'So I propose you move in here with me and we make a home together. Millie, I don't want to spend another night without you in it.'

Millie didn't hesitate. She threw herself into his lap, laughing and crying and kissing his face. 'Yes Finn. Yes to that. I don't want to spend another night without you either.'

Hanna jumped up, clapping her hands. 'Champagne Luke. Now!' She ran around the table to hug Millie, and Finn. 'We need to call Matty! Mum, can I call Matty?'

Luke returned with a bottle of champagne. The good French stuff Finn had pointed out to him earlier. While he hadn't known exactly how the night would go, he had confided in his son.

Harry held the glasses as Luke poured and then pumped Finn's hand a few times. He kissed Millie on the cheek and returned to a chair beside Hanna, holding her hand.

'Matty!' Hanna waved her phone around, she had him on FaceTime. 'You just missed the most romantic thing ever! Finn and Mum are going to, I don't know, take the next step.'

Matty laughed. 'Congratulations! And tell me, what is the next step?'

Millie took the phone and with her face close to Finn's said, 'I'm going to move in here, at the winery, with Finn.'

'Excellent!' Hanna took the phone back and chatted with her brother, then Lucas spoke to Matty, followed by Harry. 'I'll see you all at Christmas. I'm coming early this year, for Barrington Magic.'

MUCH LATER, THEIR LEGS TANGLED TOGETHER IN BED, Millie tickled his cheek with her finger. Finn turned to look at her. 'That was perfect, you know. You and me and our kids. The song was beautiful, the most romantic thing I've ever experienced.' She sighed. 'I love you, Finn.'

Finn moved closer. 'But not enough to marry me?' He said it lightly, but he had hopes that one day she would.

Leaning up on one elbow, Millie traced a finger along his collar bone, then kissed him gently. She murmured something, but he didn't think he heard it right.

'What did you say Millie?'

With a saucy smile, she turned the bedside lamp off. 'I said, be careful what you wish for, Finn Anderson.'

22

———————

Harry

Hanna held his hand all the way home and Harry wasn't sure if he should say what had been on his mind, for a long time.

'It's lovely you're so happy for your Mum, Hanna.' Harry pulled in behind her building.

'She deserves it Harry.' Hanna sighed as she walked upstairs in front of him. 'If you saw how my dad treated her, you'd know how much she deserves this. I love Finn. He's perfect for Mum.'

Once inside she headed to the kitchen. 'Water? I had a lot of champagne tonight.'

'Yes please.' Harry moved towards her room. He stayed over a few nights a week too.

Returning with their water, Hanna set the glasses down and looked around her room. 'I wonder how soon Mum will fully move out? Her room is bigger, should I move in there?'

'It sounded like she was planning to stay with Finn from tonight. But you're right, it might take time for her to fully move out.' Harry frowned for a moment. 'Can you afford the rent here, Hanna, by yourself?'

'I can. Sure.' She giggled. 'Why do you ask Harry Stewart. Do you want to move in here with me?'

Harry hadn't considered that. He sat on the bed, pulling her down beside him. 'Would you like that, Hanna Tucker?' He nuzzled her neck and she gave a sweet little moan.

Hanna pushed him away and turned up her nose. 'Maybe.' He laughed. 'But it's not a conversation for tonight. I'm thinking we could converse in a more non-verbal way.'

Harry raised his eyebrows when Hanna unzipped her dress and stepped out of it. He followed her to the bathroom, leaving his clothes in a trail behind him. With steam pouring out of the shower, she stepped in, beckoning him to follow. At that moment, Harry would follow her just about anywhere.

23

Samantha

Holding Jamie's hand, Samantha walked across the paddock to the homestead. They'd been invited for lunch and Samantha wondered if his parents knew. If it was obvious. She hadn't been to the doctor yet, that was tomorrow, but the test she'd bought had been positive.

Jamie squeezed her hand. 'They'll be happy for us, Sam. Stop worrying.'

'But we weren't going to tell anyone until I've seen the doctor.' Samantha gazed at the big house. Jamie's dad waved from the verandah.

'I don't think they know Sam, or have even guessed. But you're right, they've invited us for a reason.' Jamie's mum had called this morning and asked them to come to lunch. Usually the invitations were more casual, and just a quick text.

They went through to the big kitchen table, it's top gnarly and scarred by generations of Taits. Jill had prepared cold meats and salads. Samantha was pleased, she could pick what she wanted from the platters without making it obvious she was avoiding certain foods.

They chatted generally for a while, then Ross cleared his throat. 'You've heard about this, uh, event in town on Saturday night, for the photographers or something?'

'Yes.' Samantha looked at Jamie. They'd been talking about it last night, how they'd take the children in for the early Christmas atmosphere. 'We talked about it last night. We'll take the children in.'

'It's perfect for Evie, Dad. She's asked us a couple of times if Santa is real.' Jamie squeezed her hand. 'She's never really experienced a proper Christmas, it was all a bit chaotic last year.'

'We think so too. It will be good for both of them.' Ross looked at Jill, who added, 'we wondered if we could join you, on Saturday night. We can take our car, so we all fit in together.'

'Oh.' Sam paused, then smiled broadly. 'Oh, that would be wonderful! Yes, let's all go together. We can walk around main street and see all the windows done up.'

'And have something to eat.' Jamie chimed in and Sam giggled. *Her man loves his food.*

'And then, drive around town to see the Christmas lights? They're putting a map in the paper tomorrow of the streets that are participating.' Jill pushed the tray of cold meat closer to Samantha. 'Have some more roast lamb, Sam, you've hardly eaten anything.'

Ross leaned back, pushing his plate away. 'I'm done. Beautiful spread, love.'

'So no Christmas pudding and custard for you, Ross?' Jill stood to clear the table and Samantha quickly jumped up to help.

But Jamie was quicker. 'Stay there Sam, I'll help Mum.' He chuckled. 'Will helping get me a bigger piece of pudding?'

Jill laughed. 'I've made little individual ones, just trying out a new recipe, so they're all the same size Jamie.'

'Oh well, if you need my opinion love, I can probably squeeze one in.' Ross winked at Samantha as the others bustled into the kitchen.

The Christmas pudding was a success for Samantha. She devoured it and her tummy didn't complain. But something was going on with Ross and Jill, a sort of silent conversation passed between them. Jamie saw it too.

'Mum. Dad. What is it?' Samantha waited as Jill slid back into her chair beside Ross.

'Evie was here early this morning.' Ross seemed uncomfortable.

'She said she left something here.' Sam frowned. Ross and Jill never minded the kids coming and going.

'She has a secret.' Ross looked at Jill, who nodded. 'She confided in me and it is supposed to just be between us. Evie and me. But after she ran home, I felt I had to tell Jill. And now we need to tell you.'

'A secret? What secret?' Samantha was worried. Was something happening at school that Evie was too scared to tell her.

Jill chimed in. Ross seemed to have run out of words. 'You just said you want Evie to experience a magical Christmas?'

Samantha and Jamie nodded.

'She came over here to get Ross to help her write her letter to Santa. She didn't want to do it at school.' Jill placed her hand over her husband's. 'That she came to him, to her Pa, was pretty special.'

'She told me she's being teased.' Ross looked up. 'Did you know that she refers to Woz as her brother sometimes?'

Samantha and Jamie looked at each other and shook their heads.

'She told me she says it at school. That Woz is her brother.' Ross smiled. 'Which is really cute. And Woz doesn't seem to mind.'

'It's what we want for them. They are step-brother and sister anyway.' Jamie smiled. 'Is that what this is about? We can talk to Evie, to both of them.' The smile he gave Samantha was so full of love, that she only managed to squeak out, 'yes.'

'It's what she put in her letter to Santa.' Ross paused and Samantha could see he was feeling emotional. Instinctively she moved to his side and put her arm across his shoulders. 'In her letter to Santa.' Ross stopped and pulled a piece of paper from his pocket. 'She did a practice one, to make sure she got it right.'

He turned the piece of paper so they could all see it.

Dear Santa
Please make Jamie my Daddy so Woz will be my brother.
love
Evie Scott

Samantha's hand flew to her mouth and she stared at Jamie, before turning to Ross and sobbing loudly against his chest. He awkwardly patted her shoulder a couple of times, and then Jill was there too, and Jamie. Somehow Jamie had his arms around all of them.

After a few minutes Jill slipped back into her chair, but her hand was on Ross's arm. Jamie returned to his chair, pulling Samantha onto his lap with his arms around her.

'Oh. I had no idea she felt like this.' Samantha searched Jamie's face, trying to gain an understanding of his thoughts.

Ross cleared his throat. 'Evie's called us Pa and Nanna from the very beginning, because that's what we are to Woz.' He covered Jill's hand with his own. 'I think she truly wants to be part of this family.'

Understanding hit Samantha hard. 'She wants what Woz has. A father. And a family.' Turning, she peered up at Jamie. 'Do you think?'

Jamie spoke slowly, and the look he gave her was pure love. Samantha's heart hummed. 'But she has that, we couldn't be more of a family.'

'She still calls you Jamie, son.' Ross had a point. 'And Woz calls you, Sam.'

'The only way to fix that, once and for all …' Jamie trailed off. Samantha knew too, but it wasn't her place to say it. It had to come from Jamie.

Lifting her gently to her feet, Jamie stood up. 'We need to get married, Sam.'

'Jamie!' Jill looked shocked. 'That's not a proposal. Do it properly.'

Jamie laughed. He let her go for a moment to walk across to his father, who was on his feet too. Jamie clapped his arms around his Dad and hugged him hard. 'Love you, Dad. And you, Mum.' He reached for Samantha's hand and drew her to him. 'That Evie loves her Pa so much, she asked him to help her write this.' Jamie shook his head.

Turning to Samantha, he kissed the tip of her nose. 'I will do it properly Sam. And soon. As long as you have no doubts.'

'I've never doubted you, Jamie.' Samantha nestled against him for a moment, then threw her arms around Ross and then Jill. 'Thank you.' She would call her mum later, too.

Halfway across the paddock, on the way back to their own cottage, Samantha stopped. 'We didn't tell them our news, Jamie.'

'I thought about it for a moment.' He took her hand and they continued walking through the ankle high clover. 'But maybe that can be a surprise from Santa too.'

Samantha giggled then, and gave a tiny skip. 'A very special surprise from Santa.'

24

Freddie

For two nights after the clinic closed, Freddie worked on the window display for the Christmas magic competition. She broke open a haybale and covered the floor of the window area with hay, then set a second haybale in the centre. She cut the collie dog out of the large posters and had one leaping off the haybale with a frisbee in its mouth. She positioned the one where its tongue lolled out and the wind was in its face on the seat of child-size toy motorbike, and another one laying on the floor with its head on its paws. Using pins and double-sided tape, she placed a Santa hat on each dog.

Melanie poked her head in on the third morning and clapped her hands. 'Freddie! Well done, so cute!'

'It's not quite finished, Mel.' Freddie grinned. She had a sheet covering the window on the inside, so no one would see it until it was finished. She stepped out of the window space and held up three more posters. The first one was a cow's face, the picture taken when the cow was possibly sniffing the camera, so it's nose was huge. It was a hilarious perspective, with the other pictures of a sheep and horse taken from the same angle.

Melanie giggled. 'Oh, I can't wait to see how you position these.' The clinic door opened and the first patient arrived. 'Hello Gladys. You're here for Rusty's inoculations. Take a seat and I'll let Max know you've arrived.' Melanie sped back to reception and Freddie quickly closed the interior door to the window space.

In the afternoon, when the staff and patients had left for the day, Freddie worked on. Max offered to bring Tommy in to help, but she wanted it to be a surprise. She wrapped a large cardboard box in Christmas paper and lay it on its side, with the lid leaning against the haybale. She hung the horse, cow and sheep faces on fishing wire from the ceiling, as if they were looking into the box, and put a Santa hat on each of them. She framed the window with tinsel and a few baubles, but didn't want to detract from the central theme.

Stepping back, Freddie took in the display. She pulled the sheet in the front window to one side just long enough to dash out to the footpath and have a look from the outside. She loved it. There was just one more thing she needed to add. Rushing back inside, she covered the window again and carefully positioned a cutout of three puppies playing together in the Christmas box. She had kitten and rabbit cutouts too and she planned to change them every day.

But her biggest surprise, was that on Saturday night when everyone was in the main street to walk around and see the windows, she would exchange the cardboard cutouts for real puppies. They had three blue heeler pups at the farm she would bring in, just for a couple of hours. Callum said he'd come in too and keep an eye on them for a while so she could enjoy the celebrations in the street too. If it worked, she'd do the same on evening of the Barrington Magic Night Market. Spinning around, she clapped her hands. *Kids will love this.*

25

———

Evie (Five weeks to Christmas)

TODAY MISS ROGERS TOLD US WE'RE GOING TO SING AT the Christmas concert! The song is called *Santa Claus is coming to town*. She played it for us and I love it! I've never been to a concert.

Then she said it wasn't our usual school concert at the little hall, but on a stage at Town Hall in the main street. She said *Barrington Magic* a lot and I think she got that from Mummy.

One of the bigger girls asked if we'll have costumes and Miss Rogers said we might have to wear our school uniform. The girls all groaned, but I don't care. I think it's exciting.

I'm even more excited about tomorrow night because there's something special happening in town and we're all going in Pa's car. Jamie said there would be lights, and decorations, and lots of yummy food.

I told Mummy all about the concert and gave her the note

from Miss Rogers. She read the note and got all sad. But she said she was happy. I don't understand grown-ups, they cry when they're happy sometimes.

I COULDN'T BELIEVE IT! EVERY SHOP WINDOW WAS decorated and we ate sausages in bread right in the street outside the butcher store! Then we had a milkshake from the café and all the grown-ups had wine from the truck with Harry and Luke.

Woz and I ran around with some of the big kids from school. Charlie, Billie, Tiffany and Tommy, and Mummy didn't even watch me the whole time.

The girls, Billie and Tiffany, said they are getting tutu's made for the Christmas concert. They said I should ask Mummy to make one for me too, but I'm not really sure what it is. They said it was pretty and they're getting pink ones. I'm going to ask Mummy about it.

Everyone got three tickets with Santa's picture on them, to vote for their favourite shop window. My very favourite was the Vet's window, because of the puppies and all the animals with Santa hats. We voted for the café and the bakery too because they looked yummy. There were special boxes at the shops to put the tickets into and if you put your name on the ticket you might win a prize at the Barrington Magic night. I've never won a prize but Woz said it's probably wine or something that grown-ups like, so if I win I'll give it to mummy, or maybe Pa.

We stayed out really late and Pa drove us around the town to look at some of the houses. One had a Santa and reindeer on the roof! I know it's a fake Santa, but it looked wonderful. I hope the real Santa has read my letter.

Today has been my best day. Ever!

26

Hannelore

'The street lights are on, Mum. I'm turning our Christmas lights on too!' Hanna ran to do just that, peering outside through the café window. 'I'm happy Council blocked off the main street to vehicle traffic at six. All the vendors are setting up their food stands and there are already hundreds of people walking up and down.' She spun around, then ran across to Millie and hugged her tightly. 'It's starting to feel like Christmas!'

Millie hugged her back, then walked to the front door and propped it open. 'Come in, come in.' A group of visitors strolled inside and Millie beckoned Hanna closer. 'Run out and check on Harry and Luke. I know you want to. Then come back, I think we're going to be run off our feet shortly.'

'Are you sure?' Hanna waved to Kristen in the kitchen who had her Mum, Cathy in there, and Lucy was already taking orders at the counter. Grinning, she dived through the door, calling out, 'I won't be long.'

Loudspeakers were playing Christmas songs and the atmosphere was festive and friendly. Harry and Luke were down near the bakery on the next corner. They had an area surrounded by portable white picket fencing, as they were serving wine in plastic glasses under a special liqueur licence. There was a group of young people about her own age chatting at the back of the troop carrier where the lads had set up their bar. A bunch of older ladies had taken over a picnic table, and Hanna could see an array of food from the bakery and the butcher's sausage sizzle in front of them. And they each had a plastic cup of wine. They were talking and laughing loudly and she saw Judith and Rachael in the group but didn't recognise the others.

'Hanna!' Judith beckoned her closer. 'Meet the ladies from the Hornsby Book Club. They arrived this afternoon for tonight's celebration, and tomorrow they're coming to the book shop to meet Rose Gordon.'

'Fabulous.' Hanna smiled broadly at them. 'Welcome to Barrington. Pop down to the cafe later for eggnog and dessert.'

'Oh yes, we will, thank you.' One lady, grey-haired and spritely, leaned in as if telling a secret. Hanna stepped closer. 'But after meeting young Harry and Luke over there, we've booked a Wine for Blokes tour tomorrow afternoon.' She wiggled her eyebrows and Hanna giggled. The lady was old enough to be her grandmother.

Another woman, with bright pink hair and an impressive bosom laughed uproariously. 'We're all doing the tour luvvie, but it's not for the wine.' She suggestively bit her bottom lip and Hanna laughed so hard she almost cried.

'Has Judith told you her pet name for Harry?' Hanna winked at the pink-haired lady.

Judith chimed in. '*Hot Harry Stewart*. Since the day I met him, that's what I call him in my head.'

'And now it's in mine, Judith.' Harry had walked over and was standing right behind Judith with an open bottle of wine. 'You saucy minx.' He topped up their glasses and happily let them take selfies with him.

Walking back to their bar, Hanna nudged him. 'You've got fans, Harry Stewart.'

'Oh yes, I'm pulling in the retirees. Watch out Hanna Tucker.' Harry kissed her quickly. 'And they tip well.' Still laughing, he began to work beside Lucas.

'I'd better head back to the cafe. I'll see you later.' Hanna walked to the corner and looked back. There were two distinct customer demographics lined up at the bar. Twenty-something couples and friends, and grey-haired women in packs. She chuckled as she dashed away.

There was a mob of people at the Vet Clinic window and Hanna stopped to see what was going on. She'd admired the window earlier, the animals with Santa hats were cute and funny. She saw little Evie and Woz right at the front. Billie, Tiffany, Tommy and wee Charlie were with them. Glancing at Jamie Tait, Hanna said, 'I can't quite see. What's got them so entranced?'

Glancing down at her, Jamie mouthed *Hi Hanna* and beckoned her closer. He tapped Samantha on the shoulder and she moved aside to let Hanna in behind the children. Then she saw them. Where there had been cardboard cutout puppies earlier, there were now three fat and wriggly little blue cattle dog pups. They were playing together, rolling all over each other and chewing on the edge of the wrapped box. 'Oh, real puppies!' She clapped her hands.

Evie turned around and looked up at her. 'It really is magic, Hanna. When we came past before they weren't alive, and now they're real!' Her blue eyes were shining and Hanna's heart melted.

'That's why we call it Barrington Magic, Evie.'

Evie nodded seriously and turned back to the window. Hanna gave Samantha a quick hug. 'She's so precious Sam, truly. She's just made my night.'

Samantha's eyes glistened with unshed tears. 'Evie deserves a little bit of magic.'

'We all do, Sam.' Waving to them, Hanna jogged back to the café. People were queued out the door but no one seemed bothered. In fact, locals and visitors seemed to be mixing and chatting and Hanna decided this was the best idea ever. From the corner of her eye she saw Meggie with a camera crew heading their way, so she ran behind the counter, tying an apron on as she dashed into the kitchen.

27

Harry

IT WAS LIKE WATCHING A TRAFFIC ACCIDENT IN SLOW motion. As Lucas pulled the temporary fencing apart with his back to the main street, Harry saw Freddie walking towards him. She had her head down, focussed on something in her arms. *Puppies! Freddie is carrying puppies!*

When Freddie was less than two steps away, she looked up just as Lucas turned around. They froze and Freddie lost her grip on the dogs who tumbled from her arms, landing at her feet. They immediately waddled past Lucas towards Harry.

'Luke!' Freddie appeared simultaneously pleased and nervous.

'Freddie.' Lucas sounded grim and displeased. Freddie went bright red and shot past him to chase after the little dogs. Harry had scooped one up, but the other was cowering under the picnic table, scared by the noise, bright lights and movement all around.

Dropping to her knees, Freddie tried to coax the quivering

little pup out. Harry was about to shove the one he held into his shirt, so he could help Freddie. Lucas strode past, moved the bench seat to one side and crawled under the table, speaking softly to the puppy. It backed away, but loud laughter nearby made it stop. Edging forward, Lucas scooped the puppy up in one big hand and backed out from under the table.

Sitting on his heels for a moment, he cuddled the little dog who seemed to settle when Harry placed the other one beside it. Freddie stood up and shuffled her feet.

'Thank you, Harry.' Her words were softly spoken. 'And Luke. I was following Callum, he has the other pup with him, but I got distracted and lost him in the crowd.'

'There's another one?' Lucas stood up, still holding both dogs.

Freddie smiled then, a bit sheepishly, Harry thought. 'I exchanged the cardboard cutout puppies with real ones in the clinic window for a couple of hours. These three are ours, from the farm. Well, they're Callum's.'

'Oh, that's clever, Freddie.' Harry glanced at Lucas. 'I noticed the Clinic window was getting a lot of attention tonight, but we were too busy for me to take a closer look.'

'It was my bit of animal magic. The children loved it. I hope to do it again for the Night Market event but these little guys may be too big by then.' Freddie held her hands out to take the puppies from Lucas.

'Yes, um, good.' Lucas waited till she had them settled in her arms, then he extricated his own hands. 'Oh look, there's Callum now.'

Harry turned around. 'Hey Cal, where's the pup?'

'Hello wine blokes.' Callum grinned and patted his tummy. His shirt bulged and moved. 'This little guy was terrified by the noise and lights. Safer in here.' He turned to Freddie, taking one of the pups from her hands. 'You did well, Sis, but let's get these little guys home to their mama.' He placed an arm around Freddie's shoulders and steered her away, calling out 'bye blokes' as they went.

Harry waited for Lucas to comment. As far as he knew, that was the first time he'd seen Freddie since she came home. But Lucas stalked across to the picket fence and continued to dismantle it, setting the panels in a neat stack against the wall of the bakery.

Oh yes. Lucas still has feelings for Freddie. Harry sighed. If Lucas didn't want to comment, Harry wasn't going to start a conversation. He was way out of his depth with this stuff.

28

Finn

'Are you going to the Chamber meeting tonight Luke?' It was after five and Lucas was grubby and covered in tiny grass cuttings. 'You might need to clean yourself up a bit.' Finn grinned at his son. 'Although the grounds look great, thank you.'

'Yeah, they come up okay. But we could use some rain.' Lucas leaned the rake against the side of the ride-on mower. 'I'll put this lot away and have a quick shower. I'll go straight to the meeting and have dinner there afterwards.'

'Alright. I won't hold you up, Millie is bringing a few more things over tonight.' He shook his head, chuckling. 'I told her I could bring the delivery van and help her, you know, bring everything at once. But no, Miss independent wants to do it her way.'

Lucas nudged him. 'You don't really mind, Dad. She's been here every night since you asked her to move in. Maybe she's giving you time to make space for her stuff.'

'I've given her the small bedroom to create her own space. She's moved a bookshelf in and a big old armchair she likes to read in. And the closet is full of clothes and boxes.' Finn shrugged. 'But she's leaving a lot of stuff at the flat for Hanna to use.'

Lucas glanced at the sky suddenly. 'Do you think there's any rain in those clouds?'

Finn looked up. 'I hope so, but the weather report says not.' He jumped into the seat of the mower. 'I'll sort this, son you'd better hurry.'

MILLIE ARRIVED AND FINN CARRIED TWO BOXES OF items upstairs for her. 'This is the last of it, Finn. I'm officially living with you.' There was laughter in her tone and Finn felt a sense of happiness and anticipation he hadn't experienced in a long time.

'Living in sin, Millie.' He took the boxes into the small bedroom and set them on the floor. Turning, he took her in his arms. 'I have dinner prepared. Thai beef salad. So there's no rush. Would you like a cool drink?'

Millie snuggled against him for a moment. *Maybe the dinner can wait a lot longer?* But then she kissed him quickly and stepped back. 'A drink sounds lovely, thank you. What can I do?'

'Come and chat while I open some bubbly, I want to celebrate that you've officially moved in.' Finn took Millie's hand and strolled through to the kitchen with her.

'It feels like rain.' Millie peered out of the window, rubbing her arms with her hands. 'The temperature has dropped, oh, and there goes Luke.'

'Luke said that just before you came.' Finn dug the phone out of his pocket. 'It just says cloudy here, in the weather app.' He turned it so Millie could see.

'The weather bureau doesn't always get it right, Finn.'

They chatted quietly as they drank their first glass, then plated the salad up and moved to the dining table. Just as they finished, a large clap of thunder shook the house. 'Oh!' Millie jumped.

Finn opened the balcony door, it was fully dark now, and watched as fat drops of rain fell on the path below. 'It is rain. Hallelujah!'

Millie moved beside him, frowning for a moment. 'It sounds heavy on the roof, Finn. But I don't care, it can fill the rivers and streams and dams and tanks.' She giggled and he put his arm around her. They stayed like that for ages, watching the intermittent lightning strikes in the distance as the rain drummed down on the roof.

29

Hannelore

Shaking droplets of water from her hair, Hanna grimaced. 'I ran over the road to fetch a cardigan barely two minutes ago and the heavens opened up and dumped on me.'

'Don't complain Hanna. We need rain so badly I'm tempted to stand outside and let it soak me.' Kristen glanced at her phone, murmuring, 'Callum. He's in town, he'll join us for dinner after the meeting.'

Hanna strolled into the meeting room with Kristen and took a seat. Harry and Lucas joined her moments later, while Kristen moved to sit beside Meggie at the front of the room, opening her laptop to take the minutes.

Meggie wasted no time opening the meeting, with their Christmas event the only item on the agenda. 'Thank you for coming everyone,' she grinned, 'how about that rain?'

'The bureau got it wrong. Only last week they said we're experiencing El Nino conditions.' Ben pulled out a chair beside Meggie, nodding to those around the room. 'But if this rain continues we'll have moved straight into La Nina and they did not expect that.' Ben settled on the chair.

'That's good, though?' Hanna frowned.

'It is. But La Nina can bring floods here, more so if the catchment up in the Tops area gets the same heavy rain we're getting down here.' Ben shifted in his seat, speaking directly to Hanna. 'It's been so dry that tonight's rain should just soak in, rather than flowing downstream.'

When Ben finished, Meggie picked up her tablet. 'Tonight's special meeting is to gather feedback from Saturday's soft launch. What worked, what didn't, what do we need to improve for the actual event.' She nodded to Merv, who had raised his hand. 'One moment Merv. And I can confirm that we shot some great promo footage, the attendance was higher than expected, which bodes well for the real event. Kristen will email around the collaborative promotional opportunities later in the week.' Laying her tablet down she indicated Merv should start.

'We had a great night. Trade was good for us. On the night especially, with Wine for Blokes operating in the street next to us.' Merv held a crumpled piece of paper. 'We sold out of pies and sausage rolls on the night and by Sunday lunchtime most of the sweet stuff, like lamingtons, had gone.' He cleared his throat. 'But here's the thing. We didn't expect visitors to arrive beforehand. We were up twenty percent on Thursday and fifty percent on Friday.' Laughing, he waved the piece of paper. 'And Saturday was our biggest day ever!'

'We were booked out.' Sally from the Barrington Motel

chimed in. 'And we're already full for the main event plus bookings right through to the end of January.'

Several people spoke at once and Meggie had to slow them down so Kristen could note their comments.

'Any problems?' Meggie raised her eyebrows.

'A few people complained about parking. Out-of-towners weren't sure where to go.' Trev leaned forward. 'Do you think we could get one of the service clubs to assist with parking? You know, direct people to the public carpark behind town hall and in the side streets.'

'Good idea, Trev.' Ben scribbled something in a small notebook he withdrew from his pocket. 'We can use the car park at the oval for overflow and I think Rotary will manage that for us. I'll ask them.'

'It was a fun night for children.' Meggie nudged Ben. 'Tommy ran around with Tiffany, and Billie Murray and a couple of smaller children, looking at all the windows. They were really excited to choose their three favourites. I wonder if we could create a sort of treasure hunt for them. If they get a little map marked off by every business, they could get a goody-bag at the end.'

'Oh yes!' Hanna loved the idea. 'And most children will be accompanied by an adult, so if they participate they will visit every single shop.'

'Alright. We'll work out potential numbers and see if we can get low-cost items donated for the bags.' Meggie peered over at Kristen's laptop. 'Can you note that Kristen?'

'It doesn't have to be actual items, Meggie. What if we had vouchers too?' Hanna tapped her chin with two fingers. 'We could do something at the café, like a voucher for a coffee or milkshake. Most people will buy something else once they're in-store.'

Merv shot his hand up in the air. 'Buy-one-get-one-free vouchers. Like you Hanna, I think most people will buy more items.'

'Alright. I think we have enough here. Kristen will send out an email to members with opportunities to provide something for goody-bags, and also a link and prices for the collaborative advertising.' Meggie stood up. 'But before we finish the meeting, I'd like to recognise Hanna for the idea, and Harry for polishing it to perfection. Barrington is in good hands.'

Everyone clapped and a few shouted 'here, here' and Hanna felt herself flush. Harry seemed to take it in his stride and whispered to her, 'we're a good team Hanna Tucker.'

30

Freddie

CALLUM MET FREDDIE IN THE PUB. 'LET'S GET A BOOTH. The others should be finished with their meeting soon. What would you like to drink?'

'Soda water please, Cal.' Freddie ignored her brothers' raised eyebrows and slid into a booth for six. Callum said Harry and Hanna usually stay for dinner. And Lucas. Thinking about Lucas gave her anxiety. He hadn't been thrilled to see her on Saturday night and she was still embarrassed. But she straightened her shoulders and huffed out a breath she didn't realise she'd been holding. This is her home town. She has a right to be here, to find work, and have friends. She won't get in his way or make it difficult for him, but he can't avoid her for ever. Freddie hoped they could be civil to each other. She knew that becoming friends wasn't possible.

Callum returned with their drinks and a glass of wine for Kristen and slid into the booth beside her. 'Here they come now.'

'Hi Freddie, Cal.' Hanna bounced over to them and slid in to the seat opposite Freddie. Harry took the seat beside her and Lucas paused a few strides from their spot. He frowned at Freddie, but she smiled politely back, hoping he would see she didn't want to make trouble.

Lucas waited until Kristen was seated beside Callum, then took a drink order from Harry and Hanna and walked to the bar. Freddie felt sick to her stomach until Hanna picked up a menu from the centre of the table and shared it with Freddie. 'Pizza, Freddie? We usually get three and just share.'

Freddie nodded dumbly, peering at the menu items Hanna suggested. She tensed up when Lucas returned with the drinks but the rapid-fire discussion around the table to choose the pizzas helped her take a few normal breaths. She giggled when Hanna told Harry and Lucas there would be no red onion on any of the pizzas as her olfactory senses still haven't recovered from last time. Laughter broke the ice, and while Lucas didn't speak directly to her, he didn't ignore Freddie either.

Hanna excused herself to use the bathroom and Harry strode to the bar to get drinks. He'd asked Freddie what she wanted, but she stuck to soft drink. Callum and Kristen were deep in conversation about the weather, and how much rain it would take for the rivers to rise significantly.

Sensing Lucas watching her, Freddie turned and met his eyes. He looked uncomfortable, but when he spoke, she knew he was trying. 'The little dogs on Saturday night, did you get them home safely?'

It was a safe subject and she threw him an appreciative smile.

'Yes. One of them chewed the elastic sides of my riding boots on the way home, and now they're ruined. Little blighter.'

His tentative smile in return was brief. 'Will they be too big for the window on the big night? They look about eight weeks old.'

'Almost seven weeks, but they'll wreak havoc on the display now they've begun chewing.' Freddie glanced up as Harry and Hanna returned. 'You don't have a couple of younger puppies I can use on the night, do you Luke?'

'Puppies?' Hanna moved into the booth next to Freddie. 'That was genius, using real ones. The little kids were entranced.'

Lucas shook his head. 'I don't, Freddie.' He gave her a half smile. 'But maybe you can borrow some from a client. You're a Vet, you're sure to know if anyone has some the right age.'

The pizzas arrived then and the conversation veered between the rain and the Barrington Magic event. Freddie relaxed. She sensed the ice had been broken with Lucas and maybe they could be friends, after all.

31

——————

Evie (two weeks to Christmas)

I HAVE A PINK TUTU FOR THE CONCERT, THE SAME AS
the big girls! And pink ballet slippers. I'm so excited. We've learned
our Christmas song and a special dance. All the girls are Christmas
fairies and the boys are elves and helpers. Some of them don't
want to dress up and Miss Rogers said that's okay, they can just
wear anything they like with a Santa hat. Woz has a green shirt and
brown jeans, so he looks a bit like a Christmas tree.

We've been practising a lot as we've been inside because of the
rain. It's rained almost every day for two weeks and Pa says it's
good because all the rivers and creeks are flowing and the dams
and tanks are full. I like the noise of the rain on our roof, but
BlueDog doesn't and if there's thunder or lightning we let him
come into the laundry to sleep.

We slept up at the big house for two nights, which was really
fun. We helped Pa do his chores in the rain because he said all the

animals still need to be looked after no matter how wet it is. We wore our raincoats with hats and boots and sloshed through the mud to feed the chickens and collect the eggs, and we rode on the trailer on top of a big stack of haybales to feed hay to the springers and the horses. It was the best fun and Pa let us take turns helping him drive the tractor on the way home.

Mummy and Jamie had to go to the city. Woz said maybe they've gone to get something for us, like a motorbike. I hope he gets one from them, if Santa doesn't bring one. But I don't mind what I get as long as Santa brings what I asked him for. Then I'll know he's real.

32

Samantha

Jamie stopped twice on the way to Newcastle because Samantha was sure she was going to be sick. In the end, she wasn't, so she sipped some cool water and she watched the windscreen wipers move rhythmically in front of her as they continued their trip. She felt so washed out which made it harder to keep her condition secret from the children, and others. Jamie was driving her to a specialist doctor to check everything was alright with her and the baby. She was only about ten weeks along but felt anxious because this pregnancy was so different to her first.

Samantha had heard all about Debbie's difficult pregnancies and she agreed to the trip because Jamie was so worried. She totally got that. She wondered if Jamie's mum had guessed. Although Jill hadn't mentioned it at all, she had dropped off some dinners and offered to have the children overnight a couple of times. Samantha was grateful. Preparing meals had become problematic, as she was never sure which aroma would send her scurrying to the bathroom.

Giggling, Samantha put her hand to her mouth when Jamie began driving after their second stop.

'You're laughing Sam. Does that mean you're feeling better?' Jamie shot her a quick glance.

'I'm pretty sure your Mum has guessed. But she hasn't said anything.' Samantha sipped from her water bottle, then recapped the lid. 'Has she hinted to you?'

'Not at all, but Mum doesn't miss much. But Dad's a bit clueless about this stuff.' Jamie lay his hand on her leg for a moment. 'Even if she has guessed, she won't spoil our surprise. She'll know we'll tell them when we're ready.'

'I'm hoping after today we can feel more confident.' Tears sprang to Samantha's eyes. She'd forgotten how pregnancy hormones behaved, and wiped her eyes quickly. Jamie gave her a curious look.

'Hormones.' Samantha shrugged. 'But I do love that it is just our secret, for now.'

'Santa will have lots of surprises for our family this year.' Jamie looked pleased with himself, and Samantha nodded.

Coming to Barrington more than a year ago had changed her life. And Evie's. And maybe Woz and Jamie's too. Samantha sometimes worried that it was all too good to be true and that something bad would happen to take it all away from her. She tried to keep these thoughts at bay, but lately when she had trouble sleeping, she worried.

DRIVING HOME THE NEXT DAY, THE BACK OF THEIR CAR full of gifts to wrap and hide for Christmas, Samantha wondered again how she could be so lucky. The ultrasound showed a healthy baby of eleven weeks gestation, and while they'd opted not to know the gender, she thought she'd caught a peek but was happy to hug the knowledge to herself for a bit longer. The other good news was that the doctor was sure her morning sickness symptoms would soon abate and she'd feel much better.

Samantha must have dozed off, but woke with a start as Jamie braked and swore under his breath. Straightening in her seat she turned quickly to see why, her heart pounding.

'Sorry Sam. I didn't mean to wake you.' Jamie's face was grim as he drove slowly over the bridge on the outskirts of Barrington, on the way to the farm.

'What is it?' Samantha peered through the rain splashing against the window on her side.

'The river.' Jamie sucked in a noisy breath. 'It's almost to the bridge. It's risen a metre or more since yesterday.' He threw her a concerned look. 'If it tops the bridge we won't be able to get into town for the event on Saturday night.'

'Oh.' Tears welled in her eyes. 'Evie will be devastated. And the event will be washed out.' Pulling a tissue from the box at her feet, she blew her nose loudly. 'All that work to bring people here.' She sniffled, her heart breaking for Evie. Samantha had never seen her so excited.

'But we have rain, Sam. And the visitors will still come. But maybe not for Saturday.' Jamie changed gears as they approached their driveway. 'Will we go home first and hide the loot?' He gave her a silly grin and she nodded. 'Then we'll pick up the kids. I suspect Mum will have enough dinner for all of us, so we can eat there, catch up on the news, and then come home.'

'Tomorrow is the last day of school for the year. Do you think they'll be able to go? Evie is excited, they're having a party in the classroom.' Samantha nibbled her bottom lip. The rain was much needed, but she said a silent prayer for it not to cause floods.

'I hope so.' Jamie parked in front of their cottage. 'Stay there, I'll bring the umbrella around and take you inside.'

'I can help with the presents.' Samantha started to protest but Jamie was already at her door, umbrella in hand. They raced inside.

'I'll put my oilskin on and get everything from the car. Rest for a moment, Sam.' Jamie led her to the sofa and ensured she was settled, then kissed her soundly on the mouth. 'Back in a minute.'

33

Harry

'HAVE YOU VOTED YET, LUKE?' HARRY HELD HIS PHONE up, showing the poll from Chamber.

'No. Have you?' Lucas waved to Kristen as she carried their lunch orders across.

'Hanna's coming, we're taking a short break.' Kristen waved a hand around the café. 'It's quiet. The threat of flooding is keeping people away.'

After Hanna sat down, Harry returned to his question. 'Do we vote to cancel? What's the alternative?'

'I say no.' Hanna sounded more positive than he felt. 'We hold it anyway, for those who've made the effort to be here, including locals and business owners. It will be smaller than we hoped, but I heard Council have offered a large marquee for the main street for all the stall holders.'

'The rain has eased off.' Harry frowned. 'Although Rocky Crossing is flooded and the bridges up near Moppy, Rawdon Vale and Cobark are impassable.'

'But the way here from the coast is clear.' Kristen pointed to a chocolate brownie. 'Anyone want to share this?'

'I will.' Lucas cut the brownie in half, pushing the rest on a plate towards Kristen. 'We can't use the oval car park as it's not paved and already too wet over there.'

'We may not need it.' Hanna scooped up a scone smothered in jam and cream and handed the other half to Harry. 'There's parking behind town hall and in the side streets. And Rotary said they'd help with traffic control.'

Harry took a bite of scone, his mouth tingling when Hanna absent-mindedly thumbed a spot of cream from his top lip. He had his phone in his hand. 'The rain has eased in the last two days and they're predicting it to be patchy until after Christmas. But then there will be more coming and we're officially in La Nina. So more rain, flooded waterways, and dangerous road conditions. But maybe we'll have a short respite before it hits hard in January.'

'It has slowed Harry, but the rivers are still rising because it's still making its way down from the catchment areas.' Kristen grimaced. 'But I vote we go ahead too.' She turned her phone around. 'More than seventy percent of Chamber members have voted to push on.'

'Alright.' Harry voted yes in the poll and watched as it rose to almost eighty percent. 'But we need contingency plans. I'm staying at Hanna's from now until it's over, just in case Copeland bridge goes under. Lucy is staying too, to make sure she can help in the café.' He shot a quick look at Hanna, who nodded. 'And we've got room for you too Luke, if Finn can spare you and you don't mind the couch.'

Hanna raised her eyebrows. 'More than staying, Harry. You've moved in.'

'Oh.' Harry chuckled. 'I have become very comfortable there.'

'Every night comfortable.' Hanna laughed. 'But I'm not complaining.'

'Too funny, and yes I'll stay too, thanks Hanna.' Lucas grinned. 'What about Matty? When is he arriving from Sydney?'

'He's coming by train tonight. Harry has brought his swag in for him. Maybe Lucy should have the spare room and you and Matty can bunk in the living room.' Hanna nudged Lucas. 'It could be fun.'

'Callum and Freddie are already staying with me.' Kristen shook her head for a moment. 'Max, Meggie and Tommy are using the apartment at the clinic, just in case. Angus says he can get in, if he takes the Barrington East Road.'

'I think most business owners who live out of town will have made similar arrangements.' Harry finished his coffee and looked at his watch. 'I'm popping down to Town Hall to help set up for the concert. Jamie told me Evie is really excited about it.'

'Need a hand?' Lucas pushed his chair back. 'Although maybe I should dash home and pick up my gear. I'll stay at yours tonight Hanna and I'm happy to meet Matty at the train, if that helps?

'Nah mate. Get your stuff and pick up Matty.' Harry moved back as Kristen cleared their table. 'Hanna's working late, baking or caking or something-or-other.'

'Just working, Harry. But maybe you lads can pick up pizza and keep me a couple of pieces for later.' Hanna glanced at the counter, Lucy was beckoning to her.

Harry walked down to Town Hall, light rain dripping off his hat. Standing in the entrance, he stomped and slapped his hat against the bricks to get most of the water off before he entered the graceful old building. Peering out at the afternoon sky, he could see a few breaks in the clouds and patches of blue sky. *It will be okay. Barrington Magic, do your thing.*

34

Hannelore

THE RAIN STOPPED THE NIGHT BEFORE THE EVENT, WITH Saturday dawning bright, sunny and humid. Lots of bridges were still cut off and it would take days for some to be passable again, but Hanna sensed an atmosphere of celebration as she dashed down the street to the bakery.

The marquee hadn't been needed and most stallholders were already setting up. Stopping at the Vet Clinic window, she tapped on the glass to get Freddie's attention. She stepped outside to join Hanna.

'No luck getting another set of puppies, Freddie?' Hanna was disappointed, it had been such a lovely surprise for the children.

'No. No puppies young enough not to cause havoc.' Freddie pointed to the big Christmas box. The cardboard puppy picture had been replaced by one of three tiny kittens.

'Cute.' Hanna smiled at Freddie then caught a glint in her eye.

'Oh.' She looked back at the picture. 'You have kittens, don't you Freddie? Live kittens for later, when it all starts.' Hanna clapped and laughed out loud.

'I do. Three little ginger ones, courtesy of Mrs Tubbs. They all have new homes to go to on Xmas Day.' Freddie's pleasure was obvious and Hanna warmed to her. She really had grown up since she'd been away. She wondered if Lucas realised. 'I'm going to come to the concert, then slip them into the display before all the kids come out for the treasure hunt.' Freddie glanced over her shoulder. 'I think Harry is trying to get your attention.'

Hanna told Freddie she'd come to see the kittens later, then jogged along the street to where Harry and Lucas were setting up beside the bakery. 'Hello lads. Do you need help with anything?' Hanna stopped, watching Lucas and Matty assemble the picket fence around their site. They had two more picnic tables and a slightly bigger area than last time.

'We're all good Hanna.' Harry thrust a box of plastic glasses into her arms. 'Hold this for a moment.' He helped the others affix the last piece of fencing, then took the box from Hanna. 'Are you picking stuff up from Merv?' He jerked his head towards the bakery. 'Need a hand?'

'I'm picking up one hundred and forty little Christmas puddings. Merv let me bake them in his big bread oven, which was so much quicker than using ours.' Hanna was excited. The event had created new collaborations and Hanna saw opportunities for the future. 'I want to get them back to the café before the concert starts.' She chuckled. 'Little Evie came in with Samantha just before. She told me they left a car on this side of the creek and that Ross drove them across on the tractor, two at a time.'

Harry smiled broadly. 'That's been done before.' He tapped

her arm. 'You go and see if your puddings are ready, I'll just let Luke know that I'll carry them down for you.'

Matty had been helping out at both businesses since he'd arrived two nights ago and was going to help at the Wine for Blokes stall, although he told Hanna to message him if she needed him at the café. Millie and Finn had made it to town, and Finn was working at the café for the night. He said he'd leave the wine stand for the young ones to operate.

The street lights turned on as Hanna walked back to the café beside Harry. He carried most of the puddings in a large box, but she had a smaller lot in her own arms. 'Oh!' She stopped for a moment, as all the shop windows were illuminated. 'It's so pretty.' Christmas music was playing through speakers near Town Hall and the atmosphere was perfect.

'And look Hanna, turn around.' Harry tapped her on the shoulder, pointing back along the main street towards the road in from the city. Hundreds, if not thousands, of cars with headlights on were moving slowly along the Bucketts Way towards Barrington. In the distance she could see members of the local Rotary club, wearing hi-vis vests, directing vehicles to park.

The town had been busy all day, the street filled with locals and a lot of visitors. But this influx was amazing. 'Quick Harry.' She tried to walk faster and found the box lifted from her arms by Finn.

Harry carried his load through to the kitchen, then joined her back in the street. 'It's going to be huge Hanna. More people that we ever expected, even before the rain. I'll dash back to our stand, but if I can, I'll drop by the hall to see the kids do their thing.'

'Okay, I'll see you there.' Hanna spun around and hugged Millie as she dashed past her to the kitchen. 'They're coming,

Mum. The people, they're coming. You can see car lights for miles up the road!'

Ben Evans acted as MC, with a microphone attached to speakers outside Town Hall. He directed visitors to the information centre to get treasure maps for children and announced there would be a short presentation by local school children in the hall at six o'clock.

Just before six Millie asked if they'd manage if she and Finn ducked into the hall for the concert. Hanna had wanted to go, but the café was full. 'Go Mum, enjoy.'

A FEW CUSTOMERS DASHED OUT AFTER MILLIE, obviously going to the concert too, and Hanna wondered if she could slip away for ten minutes herself. She was about to take her apron off when a very tall and well-dressed young man entered the café.

He had the look of a grazier, wearing moleskin jeans, check shirt and riding boots. Leaning over the counter he turned on the charm and she smiled at him. 'Hello Miss. Would you know where I can find the Vet Clinic?'

'Oh, yes. On this side of the street, a bit more than halfway down.' She nibbled her lip for a moment. 'But if you're after Angus or Max, they'll be in the Town Hall right now, their kids are in the concert there.'

'Thank you.' He nodded politely, his voice smoothly modulated and strode outside. She giggled. *Private school education, with a tone like that.*

35

Freddie

FREDDIE LOCKED THE CLINIC DOOR AND STRODE DOWN to the Town Hall. The kittens were happily curled up on a blanket in the large Christmas box, and she'd left them two small balls of wool to play with.

She didn't see Bart stride into the café as she slipped inside the hall. She watched the younger children sing *Santa Claus is coming to town* and do a little dance. One little girl, Evie, had cowboy boots on with her tutu, but others wore ballet slippers. She was the cutest thing, smiling gaily the whole time. Laughing, clapping and cheering with the crowd, Freddie was about to slip out through the side door when Matty found her.

'Someone's looking for a Vet, Freddie. I said I'd get you, rather than Max or Angus.' He jerked his head towards the stage. 'Their kids are up next.'

Freddie followed him out through the side door. 'Do you

know what he, or she, needs?' Freddie strode quickly beside Matty.

'He. Horse problem I think. Looks like a rich farmer lad.' Matty shrugged his shoulders. 'Way above my pay grade, Freddie.'

'Okay.' They were nearly at the clinic where a small crowd had gathered. She noted the kittens were still playing happily. She raised her eyebrows at Matty, who looked at people in the crowd but shook his head.

'He might be at Wine for Blokes. That's where he spoke to us.' Matty pushed on, the pavement was crowded with people, families mostly, and laughing children darting in and out with treasure maps in their hands. *Clever Hanna and Harry.*

'Oh, there he is. Talking to Luke.' Matty pointed and Freddie peered ahead, then stopped in her tracks. *Bloody Bart Sterling. What the hell is he doing here?*

Matty bumped into her. 'Hey, Freddie!' Bart and Lucas looked up, and seeing Freddie, Bart strolled towards her, smiling. She tried to see Lucas, but he turned his back, getting something out of the large cooler under the bar table. Harry was chatting with customers.

Freddie began to backpedal and the smile on Matty's face froze as he looked from her to Bart and back. 'Freddie?'

Bart stopped in front of her, clamped his giant hands on her shoulders and drew her in for a hug. She stiffened. He bent to kiss her and she turned her head. 'No. No. No. Bart, what the bloody hell are you doing here? In Barrington?'

'I came to see you, Freddie.' He spoke smoothly, one arm now slung across her shoulders. 'Have you missed me? I've missed you.'

Through gritted teeth Freddie snarled as she twisted away,

removing his arm violently. 'You've been sent to get the horse trailer from Scone, haven't you?'

Bart leaned back against the wall of the Trev's shop, confidence oozing from every cell. 'Not sent. I volunteered. Thought I could drop by and visit you first.'

'Oh, really? And where does your fiancée think you are?' Freddie stepped back, almost toppling a small child rushing by. 'Sorry!' She called after the little boy.

'Come on Freddie. I'm getting married soon. We can have a bit of fun, I'm staying at the motel.' He suddenly straightened and grabbed her arm, snarling quietly. 'You little prick tease, I've come all this way.'

Spinning around, Freddie caught his chin with her elbow. There were so many people in the street that she didn't want to make a scene. 'Take your hands off me Bart. I'm too good for the likes of you. Check out of your room and go and get that trailer because you're not welcome here. You're not my type, at all.' Her voice was quiet, her tone steely.

Bart's face changed then, and Freddie stepped back. She knew he had a bad temper and despised not getting his way. He tried to grab her again but she stepped out of reach.

'Actually Bart, I should thank you.' Freddie kept her distance.

'Why?' He paused, his face red with barely-controlled anger.

'Because getting caught up with you, shone a light on the type of man you really are. You're no match for the man of my heart. He's a better man than you in every way possible.' Freddie sensed Matty was standing near her, but she didn't care. He was a friend and he'd step in if she needed him to. She knew that.

'Oh really?' Bart snorted. 'So who is this man? This better man?' He glared at her.

'His name is Lucas.' Freddie put her hands on her hips. 'Bart Sterling, you're not even good enough to shine his boots.' Freddie saw Bart's demeanour change as his anger was further roused. Worried, she stepped back. She looked around for Matty, or Harry, but there were only strangers rushing along the street.

Reaching for her, Bart snarled. 'Where is he now, Freddie?' She tried to step away, looking over her shoulder to make sure she wouldn't bump another child as she moved back.

'He's right here.' Lucas stepped between them, and while he wasn't as broad as Bart, he was almost as tall. Bart hesitated and Freddie wanted to rush back in, worried he'd punch Lucas.

'And I'm Harry, and this is Matty.' Harry appeared beside her and Matty hovered beside Lucas. Bart shook his fist at her, spat out a few expletives, and turned away, quickly disappearing into the crowd. Freddie hoped she'd never see his face again.

Tears swam in her eyes and she knew her face would be flushed bright red, but she kept her chin up as she murmured grateful thanks to Harry and Matty.

'We've got customers Freddie, will you be okay?' Harry patted her shoulder when she nodded and jogged back to their stand. Matty followed him.

Turning, Freddie came face to face with Lucas. She wasn't sure how much he'd heard, or if he was just protecting her as a friend. He didn't look pleased, but he stepped closer and gave her a gentle hug. 'There are things to be said, Freddie Campbell, but not right now.' She smiled tremulously, then stared after him, speechless, as he returned to his stall.

Slipping inside the Clinic, Freddie carefully lifted one of the kittens out of the display and cuddled it in her lap in the darkened waiting room, while she cried silent tears. *Could it be possible that Luke still had feelings for her?* Yes, there are things to be said.

36

———————

Samantha

SAMANTHA CRIED WHEN EVIE WAS UP ON STAGE. SEEING her laughing and dancing, even if she did spin the wrong way a couple of times, was beautiful. Her little daughter seemed to entrance a lot of people and Samantha imagined she could feel the Barrington Magic, right there in the town hall.

They stayed to watch the older children perform. Evie wanted to see 'the big girls' who wore tutu's just like hers. They'd had a moment earlier in the evening, when Ross had taken them across the flooded creek on the tractor. Evie was wearing her cowboy boots and insisted on holding her ballet slippers, but she somehow dropped them in the rushing water and they disappeared in moments.

Evie had cried loudly, until Ross had whispered something to her. After that she didn't seem to mind. Miss Rogers told her she could perform in bare feet but Evie insisted on wearing the boots, and no one seemed to care. It made her stand out, and twice as cute in the performance. At least Samantha thought so.

At the end of the concert, Ben Evans announced the winning Christmas window displays. Barrington Vet came first and Angus and Max rushed forward, collecting their trophy together. The Bakery came second and the hardware store third. Everyone clapped loudly. Then Ben drew one vote slip randomly out of a huge bucket, which was for a weekend stay in Barrington at The Lofts, a Wine for blokes Tour, breakfast at the café and dinner at the pub. An older lady with bright pink hair moved forward to claim it, laughing loudly as she did.

Christmas Eve

'THEY'RE FINALLY ASLEEP.' Samantha moved into Jamie's arms, as he put his boots on at the back door. 'Woz is on the trundle bed in Evie's room, it was the only way they'd settle.'

Grinning, Jamie looked down at her as he reached for his oilskin. It was raining again, but not hard. 'I'm going to bring the reindeers through now.'

'I want to come.' Samantha reached for her own coat.

'It's wet out there Sam, stay here and keep dry, it won't take me long.' Jamie held her face in his enormous hands and kissed her mouth softly. She quivered. Sometimes the strength of his love took her by surprise.

'No. I want to be part of it. I'm coming.' She handed him her coat, giving him a you-can't-tell-me-what-to-do look. Jamie sighed and held her coat so she could turn around and slide her arms in. She slipped her feet into gumboots and followed him outside.

Hand in hand, with Jamie carrying a torch, they walked across to the small paddock near the house. He'd left three horses there earlier that day. Jamie whistled quietly and Captain raised his head, nickered once, and trotted across to the gate. The two mares followed and Jamie removed the lead ropes that had been loosely tied to the gate, clipping them to the halters of the three horses. 'You take your Misty, Sam and I'll lead Captain and the other.'

The walked back to the house, Samantha behind Jamie and his horses. He opened the gate into their back garden and closed it once they were through. 'Can you hold their leads while I get the bale of hay from the garden shed?'

Despite the rain dripping from her hat onto her neck, Samantha giggled. 'This is so much fun.'

Jamie carried the haybale of fresh lucerne to the middle of the back yard, cut the strings and removed them, then spread a little bit out. 'Okay. Unclip them all.'

Samantha removed the leads and the horses trotted straight to the hay, snuffling and munching quietly. Jamie picked up a hay biscuit and moved it further away, and Captain followed him. 'Alright Sam, let's go and sit on the back porch out of the rain. I'll make a pot of tea for us.'

Slipping out of her coat and hat, Samantha shook a few droplets from her hair once under the shelter the verandah afforded. It wasn't cold, just wet. Jamie returned with a mug of hot chocolate for her and a beer for himself.

Raising her eyebrows, she took the cup and sipped. 'What happened to tea?' She sipped again. 'But this is better.'

'Santa has a beer when he drops by. But I thought an elf helper might have a hot chocolate.' Jamie's face was alight and she could feel his enjoyment wash over her.

They stayed side by side on the porch for more than an hour. The horses quietly moved around the yard, eating the hay. As Samantha watched, one of the mares lifted her tail, depositing a steaming mound of manure near the clothesline.

'Aaah. Reindeer poop. Excellent.' Jamie laughed out loud, then clapped a hand to his mouth.

Giggling, Samantha stood up. 'I'll just check they're still asleep.'

Ten minutes later Jamie was back in his oilskin and had the lead ropes clipped on. 'Stay this time, Sam. I'll just let them back into their paddock.' Samantha agreed, and stood up, her empty mug in one hand and the beer bottle in the other. It wasn't empty. She held it out to Jamie but he shook his head. 'Santa doesn't like to get drunk, so he leaves a bit in the bottle.' Samantha laughed, delighted.

When Jamie returned, Samantha had set the half empty bottle and the unwashed mug on a wooden tray on the kitchen table. She put a slice of fruitcake with it. 'Is this right?'

'Yep. I'll just leave this little scrap of hay near the chimney and if you grab a carrot, I'll bite the end off.' Jamie placed the hay down, pushing a few wisps close to the Christmas tree, where a few presents already lay. These were the ones they'd bought for the children themselves and set under the tree days ago. Samantha had been impressed that the kids had looked at them, and even picked them up, but hadn't tried to unwrap them.

Samantha fetched the carrot, watching in amazement as Jamie nibbled one end then lay it near the hay. 'Rudolph sometimes comes inside with Santa.' His explanation made her chuckle.

'Alright, I'll message Dad. He'll drive the presents down now. We'll have to be quiet.' Jamie peeked into Evie's room as they walked to the front door. Samantha could see both children were fast asleep before he closed the door.

Headlights appeared, then disappeared as Jamie's father turned the car around, backing it right up to the front verandah. With the rear door open they could move the gaily wrapped presents inside as quietly as they could. Ross hugged Samantha, but didn't say a word. In fifteen minutes he was gone, whispering that they'd come down before breakfast to see the kids open their presents. Tracey, Samantha's mum, had arrived on the same train as Matty two nights ago, but she was staying in the homestead with Ross and Jill.

Before she fell asleep in Jamie's arms, Samantha acknowledged to herself that this was her best Christmas, Ever.

It was barely six when Evie and Woz launched themselves onto their bed, laughing and calling out 'Santa came, Santa came!' Jamie moved his arm quickly to protect Samantha's tummy from Evie's knee as she bounced onto the bed.

Jamie messaged his father and by the time they were dressed, the grandparents had arrived by car. The rain had stopped overnight but the paddock between their homes was wet. Ross, Jill and Tracey kicked off their footwear and padded into the cottage in their socks. Ross hauled in a bag of presents, Jill carried a platter of mini quiches and Tracey had a sealed container of something, possibly cake.

Entranced by the remnants of Santa's snack, the children were excited and noisy. They raced around the living room, touching packages and trying to read labels. Samantha boiled the jug and Jamie joined her at the kitchen sink, peering through the window.

'Oh!' Jamie spoke loudly. 'Something has been in the garden.'

Evie and Warwick flew into the room. 'What? What can you see?'

'Let's take a look.' Jamie led them through the laundry, instructing them to put their gumboots on. Samantha and the grandparents watched from the back verandah as Jamie, still holding their hands, walked them around the yard.

'Hoof prints Evie! Hoof prints!' Warwick cried out. Samantha watched Evie peer cautiously where Warwick was pointing, then she screwed up her nose.

'Ew! Poop. Mummy there's poop here.' Evie stepped back.

'It's reindeer poop, Evie. And reindeer footprints.' Woz ran around in a circle.

Evie stared at Sam, then Jamie. 'Really?' Jamie scooped her into his arms and strode around the yard, Woz gambolling beside them.

'I left a bale of lucerne hay here last night, Just in case they were hungry.' Jamie turned around in a circle. 'But there's hardly any left. And there are lots of hoof prints.'

'Reindeer.' Woz tugged at Evie's shirt. 'Like I told you Evie.'

Evie began to giggle, then laugh, her skinny arms tight around Jamie's neck. 'Reindeer. We had reindeer in our yard.' Jamie held her close and took Warwick by the hand, leading them back to the house.

'I think so, but who is going to clean up the reindeer poop?' He gazed at Samantha over Evie's head and she blinked away tears.

'You can!' The children shouted together and pointed at Jamie who pretended to be horrified, until laughing, they trooped inside to open their gifts.

37

Evie (Christmas Day)

IT WAS THE BEST CHRISTMAS DAY, EVER! WOZ AND I found reindeer poo in our back yard, and Santa ate most of the snacks we left, although he didn't drink all the beer and Pa said Santa doesn't drink and drive.

Nanna and Tee (Mummy's Mum), gave us something to eat and we each opened a present. There were some that Mummy bought, because they were under the tree all week, but I could see something big behind the Christmas tree. When we'd opened just about everything, Woz was allowed to get that one and Pa had to help him. It was a motorbike, just like he'd asked Santa for. They even let him start it up, right in the lounge room.

But I couldn't see a present for me, from Santa. I felt like crying but only for a moment, because Jamie suddenly wriggled in his chair and said something was digging into him and could I help him.

I pushed my hand down behind him and found something small. A little box wrapped in gold paper. I gave it to Jamie and he said it was for him from Santa. He seemed really confused and I was disappointed because I thought only kids got Santa presents. But then he got excited because Santa had written him a note. I didn't want to spoil it for him, so I sat beside Mummy as he unwrapped it.

And that's when the magic happened!

Jamie slid off his chair and kneeled in front of Mummy and me. Mummy cried a little bit, I still don't know why adults do that if they're happy, but I just held my breath. Then Jamie said he loves Mummy and me and he asked us to marry him. Mummy said yes straight away. Jamie put the sparkling ring from the box on her finger and everyone cheered. Except me.

I told him I still had one question. Jamie sat beside Mummy and Woz hopped on the sofa too. Everybody was quiet, so I didn't have to say it very loudly.

'Can I call you Daddy now?'

Jamie, I mean Daddy, said yes and that's how I know that Santa is real.

EPILOGUE

Samantha

They spent the Christmas Day afternoon at Barrington Ridge Wines with all their friends. The water had receded enough for most people to get there. Evie and Woz played cricket and hide-and-seek with the bigger kids and by the time the barbecue was ready they were grubby and muddy, but happy.

Samantha loved the look of pride on Jamie's face when Evie announced to everyone that he was her Daddy. Woz continued to call her Sam and she didn't mind if he never called her Mummy, as long as he knows she loves him.

Meggie sat with Samantha after that and raised her eyebrows when Sam declined the champagne she offered. Meggie asked about their wedding plans and Sam didn't have any, except Jamie said he'd like to do it as soon as possible. Meggie suggested the Winery as a venue and Samantha gazed around with fresh eyes.

She'd though they'd do something low key at the homestead, but it was beautiful here.

Finn played his guitar and sang for them after dinner, until Lucas took the guitar and told him to enjoy himself, then played music through the speakers. A country song came on and Harry, Hanna and all the young ones did a line dance and next thing they were teaching it to everyone, even her Mum and Jill. Samantha didn't think she'd ever heard so much laughter in one place. She wiped her eyes surreptitiously with a tissue. *Pregnancy hormones.*

Finding herself observing and not drinking, Samantha noticed how Lucas and Freddie moved away to sit by themselves for a while. They seemed to talk for a long time and later Lucas danced with Freddie in his arms.

Sitting with Nicole, Jill and her Mum, Samantha realised she no longer felt the changes in the last eighteen months were too good to be true. She was relaxed and felt at home in this town, with these people.

The evening was drawing to an end and Samantha stood when Jamie gave her a should-we-take-the-kids-home-now look. He'd already put the esky and containers she'd brought, now empty of food, in the car.

Suddenly Ross called out. 'Congratulations Jamie and Sam!' Everyone cheered and gathered around and Samantha had an overwhelming desire to share *all* of their news.

'Evie! Woz!' Samantha beckoned them closer. Clearing her throat Samantha called out, 'excuse me everyone, before you go, there's one more thing.'

Watching them, raising eyebrows and grinning, their faces expectant, Samantha thought many had wondered. But the children didn't know and she wanted this day to be perfect. 'Jamie and I have more news.' Her tears began flowing, she couldn't help it, so she nudged Jamie to continue.

'Some of you may have guessed, but in case you haven't, we're having a baby.' Jamie's chest seemed to expand, standing with one large hand on Warwick's shoulder. Everyone began speaking at once, congratulating them and asking the kids what they thought.

But Woz had the last word. 'Now that Evie is my sister, I vote we have a boy-baby.' Samantha wrapped her arms around Jamie, her heart bubbling with happiness. Evie slipped her hand into her brother's and they ran across to Pa and Nanna and Tee together.

Touching her tummy for a moment, Samantha met Jamie's eyes and whispered, 'Barrington Magic.'

THE END

ACKNOWLEDGMENTS

Big thanks to my fabulous reader/proof-reader, Tanya M, who has been with me from the very beginning.

A huge shout-out to my girls Emily and Jasmine for always being on *Team Susan*. Your absolute belief in me lifts me when I'm feeling low. And to Bloke for your unwavering support. Always grateful for all you do.

Thank you to my writing group: Phillipa, Michelle and Heather. Your support, guidance, and friendship are a blessing (and often a source of hilarity!) Without you, I would not have had the courage to give up my day job and do this writing-editing thing full-time.

The generosity of the authors I've met warms my heart. I've had fabulous author gigs with Julie, Cathryn, Heather, Fiona and create the RWAus magazine with Helen, Jan and Tanya every month. I've attend the RWAus conference for the last two years - and am thrilled to be a 2025 RuBY Winner for The Barrington Book Club.

Thank you to my ARC team for your early reviews - you're all so amazing.

To Trudy Schultz and Angie White for your photography, and to Lorna for your friendship, free accommodation and help at the markets when I'm in your area. And to Debbie, for your fifty years of friendship.

Lastly — thank you book lovers — for reading my words, writing reviews and recommending my books. Without you, there'd be no words.

SUSAN MACKIE

*Author of **The Barrington Book Club - 2025 RUBY Award Finalist** (Romance Writers of Australia award).*

A voracious reader, Susan dreamed of becoming a writer from the age of eight. Career advisors told her it wasn't a real thing and suggested journalism. So she became a journalist, then took a zig-zag path to publish her first book in 2020, via a varied career in publishing, marketing, tourism and small business. Susan even worked in State Government for a few years (but she doesn't talk about that much).

Nervous about the release of Charlie's Will, she told Bloke while sitting on the sofa one night, that she'd be happy if she sold fifty. Charlie's Will quickly reached Number One in its genre on Amazon - motivating Susan to crack on with more stories and take her writing seriously. Finally. Now Susan is a happy Indie Publisher and offers services to other writers (editing, formatting). She is also the publisher of the Love in a Sunburnt Land Anthology series, co-authored with four (quite brilliant) Aussie women.

Susan loves engaging with fellow authors and readers, and she discovered something she thought was kinda funny. A lot of authors tell her they're introverted. It's a writerly thing, apparently. But (and here's the funny bit), Susan isn't. Introverted. Not one bit. Not at all. Speaking and presenting at writers festivals, conferences and libraries is totally her thing.

So it's okay to send Susan a message, ask a question and chat on social media. She thrives on it and will always respond. Send her a photo of one of her books 'in the wild' and she'll share it. Everywhere.

If you enjoyed this book, join our Facebook group - The Barrington Book Club - and visit Susan's website on the link below.

www.susanmackie.com

ALSO BY SUSAN MACKIE

Coffee is my Calling (short prequel)

Charlie's Will

A Place to Start Over

Ragged Mountain Ranges (novella)

The Bee Whisperer

Meggie & Max (novella)

Something in the Water (novella)

The Barrington Book Club

The Secret Reader

One Good Man

www.ingramcontent.com/pod-product-compliance
Lightning Source LLC
Chambersburg PA
CBHW061452210726
48287CB00007B/2475

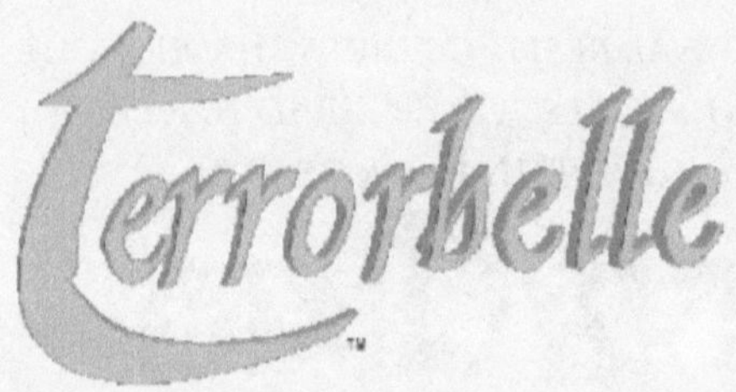

HALF OGRE & HALF PIXIE, THIS FORMER DAEMOR MOVED TO NEW YORK TO WORK FOR NEMESIS & CO. TO CONTINUE THE FIGHT AGAINST INJUSTICE.

JESTER TO KING ARTHUR, KNIGHT OF THE ROUND TABLE, SIR DAGONET WAS THE FIRST KNIGHT TO ENCOUNTER THE HOLY GRAIL. CAMELOT IS GONE, BUT DAGONET LIVES THROUGH THE AGES UPHOLDING A FORGOTTEN CODE OF

HEX WAS BORN A MAGÍ, A MAGE WITH THE ABILITY TO USE EVERY KIND OF MAGIC. CURSED WITH PAIN AND WORSE FOR USING HIS POWERS, HEX DARES TO STAND BETWEEN THE INNOCENT AND THE CREATURES OF DARKNESS–WHETHER THEY BE VAMPYRES, DEMONS, HEAVY METAL MAGES, OR THE DEVIL HIMSELF. WHEN FACING THOSE WHO CAN MAKE YOU CURSE THE NIGHT, SOMETIMES THE ONLY WAY TO SURVIVE IS TO ASK FOR HELP. THE LEGEND OF THE MAN YOU ASK IS CALLED

DAUGHTER OF NIGHT, GODKILLER, ENFORCER FOR THE COUNCIL OF THRONE. NEMESIS HAS MANY TITLES, BUT ONLY ONE MISSION– PUNISH THE GUILTY.

THEY ARE THE FORGOTTEN CHILDREN, CAST OFF BY SOCIETY. SAVED FROM THE STREETS, THEY HAVE FOUND A HOME WITH LEGENDS.

PADWOLF PUBLISHING BOOKS BY PATRICK THOMAS

***THE MURPHY'S LORE*™ SERIES**

TALES FROM BULFINCHE'S PUB

FOOLS' DAY: *A Tale From Bulfinche's Pub*

THROUGH THE DRINKING GLASS: *Tales From Bulfinche's Pub*

SHADOW OF THE WOLF: *A Tale From Bulfinche's Pub*

REDEMPTION ROAD

BARTENDER OF THE GODS: *Tales From Bulfinche's Pub*

***THE MURPHY'S LORE AFTER HOURS*™ UNIVERSE**

NIGHTCAPS - *AFTER HOURS Vol. 1*

EMPTY GRAVES - *AFTER HOURS Vol. 2*

FAIRY WITH A GUN: *The Collected Terrorbelle*™

FAIRY RIDES THE LIGHTNING: *a Terrorbelle*™ *novel*

DEAD TO RITES: *The DMA Casefiles of Agent Karver*™

LORE & DYSORDER: *The Hell's Detective*™ *Mysteries*

***MURPHY'S LORE STARTENDERS*™**

STARTENDERS

CONSTELLATION PRIZE

***MURPHY'S LORE AFTER HOURS* Books by Patrick Thomas & John L. French**

RITES OF PASSAGE: *A DMA Casefile of Agent Karver and Detective Bianca Jones*

BULLETS & BRIMSTONE a Mystic Investigators™ book

featuring Hell's Detective & Bianca Jones

FROM THE SHADOWS a Mystic Investigators™ book
featuring The Nightmare, Nemesis & The Pink Reaper™

Other Mystic Investigators*™ *books
MYSTIC INVESTIGATORS
ONCE MORE UPON A TIME *by Patrick Thomas & Diane Raetz*

OTHER BOOKS

NEW BLOOD edited by Diane Raetz & Patrick Thomas

DEAR CTHULHU*™ *Series

HAVE A DARK DAY

GOOD ADVICE FOR BAD PEOPLE

CTHULHU KNOWS BEST

THE JACK GARDNER MYSTERIES

THE ASSASSAINS' BALL